DATE DUE

FIGHTING RUBEN WOLFE

GO THERE.

OTHER TITLES AVAILABLE FROM PUSH

FIGHTING RUBEN WOLFE

MARKUS ZUSAK

PUSH

SCHOLASTIC INC.

NEW YORK   TORONTO   LONDON   AUCKLAND   SYDNEY

MEXICO CITY   NEW DELHI   HONG KONG   BUENOS AIRES

SPECIAL THANKS TO

CELIA JELLETT FOR HER KINDNESS, COMMITMENT, AND EXPERTISE

VIC MORRISON FOR ALL THE CHALLENGES

Original American hardcover edition published by Arthur A. Levine Books, an imprint of Scholastic Press, February 2001

for Scout

FIGHTING RUBEN WOLFE

CHAPTER 1

The dog we're betting on looks more like a rat.

"But he can run like hell," Rube says. He's all flannelette smiles and twisted shoes. He'll spit, then smile. Spit, then smile. A nice guy, really, my brother. Ruben Wolfe. It's our usual winter of discontent.

We're at the bottom of the open, dusty grandstand.

A girl walks past.

Jesus, I think.

"Jesus," Rube says, and that's the difference, as both of us watch her, longing, breathing, being. Girls like that don't just show up at the dog track. The ones we're used to are either chain-smoking mousy types or pie-eating horsy types. Or beer-drinking slutty types. The one we watch, however, is a rare experience. I'd bet on her if she could run on the track. She's great.

Then there's only the sickness I feel from looking at legs I can't touch, or at lips that don't smile at me. Or hips that don't reach for me. And hearts that don't beat for me.

I slip my hand into my pocket and pull out a ten-buck note. That should distract me. I mean, I like to look at girls a bit, but it always ends up hurting me. I get sore eyes, from the distance. So all I can do is say something like, "So, are we puttin' this money on or what, Rube?" as I do on this grayish day in this fine lecherous city of home.

"Rube?" I ask again.

Silence.

"Rube?"

Wind. Rolling can. Bloke smoking and coughing close behind. "Rube, are we betting or not?"

I hit him.

A backhander.

To my brother's arm.

He looks at me and smiles again.

He says, "Okay," and we look for someone to con into placing our bet for us. Someone over the age limit. It's never hard around here. Some old bloke with half his

2

crack pouring out the back of his trousers will always put one on for you. He might even ask for a share of the winnings, if the pooch you bet on wins, that is. However, he'll never find you — not that we would leave him out anyway. You have to humor those poor old alcoholic please-don't-let-me-turn-out-like-him sort of fellas. A cut of the winnings isn't going to hurt them. The trick is to win something at all. It hasn't happened yet.

"C'mon." Rube stands up, and as we walk, I can still see that girl's legs in the distance.

Jesus, I think.

"Jesus," Rube says.

At the betting windows we encounter a small problem.

Cops.

What the hell are they doin' here? I wonder.

"What the hell are *they* doin' here?" Rube says.

The thing is, I don't even hate cops. To tell you the truth, I actually feel a little sorry for them. Their hats. Wearing all that ridiculous cowboy gear around their waists. Having to look tough, yet friendly and approachable at the same time. Always having to grow a mustache (whether male, or in some cases, female) to look

3

like they have authority. Doing all those push-ups and sit-ups and chin-ups at the police academy before they get a licence to eat doughnuts again. Telling people that someone in their family just got mangled in a car wreck . . . The list just goes on and on, so I'd better stop myself.

"Look at the pig with the sausage roll," Rube points out. He clearly doesn't care that these cops are hanging around like a bad smell. No way. It's actually the exact opposite, as Rube walks straight toward the cop with the mustache who is eating a sausage roll with sauce. There are two of them. There's the sausage roll cop and a female cop. A brunette, with her hair tied under her hat. (Only her bangs fall seductively to her eyes.)

We arrive at them and it begins.

Ruben L. Wolfe: "How y' feelin' today, constable?"

Cop, with food: "Not bad, mate, how are you?"

Rube: "Enjoyin' that sausage roll, are y'?"

Cop, devouring food: "Sure bloody am, mate. You enjoyin' watchin'?"

Rube: "Certainly. How much are they?"

Cop, swallowing: "A buck eighty."

Rube, smiling: "You got robbed."

Cop, taking bite: "I know."

Rube, starting to enjoy himself: "You should haul that tuckshop in for that, I reckon."

Cop, with sauce on edge of his lip: "Maybe I should haul you in instead."

Rube, pointing at sauce on lip: "What for?"

Cop, acknowledging sauce on lip and wiping it: "For plain smart aleck behavior."

Rube, scratching his crotch conspicuously and glancing at the female accomplice cop: "Where'd y' pick *her* up?"

Cop, beginning to enjoy himself now as well: "In the canteen."

Rube, glancing at her again and continuing to scratch: "How much?"

Cop, finishing sausage roll: "A buck sixty."

Rube, stopping the scratching: "You got robbed."

Cop, remembering himself: "Hey, you better watch it."

Rube, straightening his ragged flanno shirt and his pants: "Did they charge you for sauce? On the sausage roll, that is."

Cop, shifting on spot: nothing.

Rube, moving closer: "Well?"

Cop, unable to conceal the truth: "Twenty cents."

Rube, staggered: *"Twenty cents! For sauce?"*

Cop, obviously disappointed in himself: "I know."

Rube, earnest and honest, or at least one or the other: "You should have just gone without, out of principle. Don't you have any self-control?"

Cop: "Are you tryin' to start somethin'?"

Rube: "Certainly not."

Cop: "Are y' sure?"

At this point, the accomplice brunette female cop and I exchange looks of embarrassment and I consider her without her uniform. To me, she is only wearing underwear.

Rube, answering the cop's question: "Yes sir, I'm sure. I'm not trying to start anything. My brother and I are just enjoying this wonderfully gray day here in the city and admiring the speedy beasts on their way around the track." A showbag, he is. Full of garbage. "Is that a crime?"

Cop, getting fed up: "Why are you talking to us anyway?"

Female accomplice cop and I look at each other. Again. She has nice underwear. I imagine it.

Rube: "Well, we were just . . ."

Cop, testy: "Just what? What do you want?"

Female cop looks great. Brilliant. She's in a bath. Bubbles. She rises up. She smiles. At me. I shake.

Ruben, grinning loudly: "Well, we were hoping you might put a bet on for us. . . ."

Female cop, from the bath: "Are you kidding?"

Me, smashing my head up through the water: "Are you bloody jokin', Rube?"

Rube, smacking my mouth: "My name's not Rube."

Me, back in reality: "Oh, sorry, James, y' tosser."

Cop, holding scrunched-up sausage roll bag with sauce smothered inside it: "What's a tosser?"

Rube, distressed: "Oh God almighty, this can't be happening! How ridiculously stupid can one man be?"

Cop, curious: "What *is* a tosser?"

Female accomplice cop, who is about five foot nine and uses the police gym I'd say four nights a week: "You look at one every morning in the mirror." She's tall and lean and great. She winks at me.

Me: speechless.

Rube: "That's the way, love."

Female unbelievably sexy cop: "Who you callin' love, lover boy?"

Rube, ignoring her and going back to ignorant don't-even-know-what-a-tosser-is cop: "So will you put a bet on or not?"

Tosser cop: "What?"

Me, to all of them but not loud enough: "This is downright bloody ridiculous." People mill around and past us, to place bets.

Female accomplice cop, to me: "You wanna taste me?"

Me: "Love to." It's my imagination, of course.

Tosser cop: "Okay."

Rube, shocked: *"What?"*

Tosser cop: "I'll put the bet on for y's."

Rube, floundering: "Really?"

Tosser cop, trying to impress: "Yeah, I do it all the time, don't I, Cassy?"

Hundred percent pure female cop, clearly *unim*pressed: "Whatever y' reckon."

Me: "Is that ethical?"

Rube, incredulous, to me: "Are you mentally challenged?" (He's recently become tired of the word *spastic*. He reckons the new way makes him sound more sophisticated. Something like that, anyway.)

Me: "No, I'm not. But —"

All three of them, to me: "Shut up." The bastards.

Tosser cop: "What's the dog's number?"

Rube, happy with himself: "Three."

Tosser cop: "Its name?"

Rube: "You Bastard."

Tosser cop: "Pardon?"

Rube: "I swear it. Here, look at our program."

We all look.

Me: "How'd they get away with a name like that?"

Rube: "It's 'cause today's just a lot of amateur stuff. Anything with four legs'll get a run. It's a wonder there aren't any poodles out there." He glances at me seriously. "Our fella can run but. Take my word for it."

Tosser cop: "Is that the one that looks more like a rat?"

Accomplice gorgeous cop: "But he runs like hell, they reckon."

In any case, while the tosser cop takes our money,

walks away, throws his sausage roll bag in the bin and makes the bet, the following things happen: Rube smiles incessantly to himself, the accomplice cop has her hands on her honey hips, and I, Cameron Wolfe, imagine making love to her in my sister's bed of all places.

It's disagreeable, isn't it?

Yet.

What can you do?

When the cop comes back, he says, "I put ten on 'im myself."

"You won't be disappointed." Rube nods, accepting our ticket. Then he says, "Hey, I think I'm gonna turn you in for this puttin' bets on for minors. It's a dis-grace."

(In all the time I've known him, my brother has never said just simple *disgrace*. He has to say it in two parts. *Dis* and *grace*. "Dis-grace.")

"So what?" the cop says. "And besides . . . who y' gonna tell?"

"The cops," Rube answers, and we all smirk a little, and head for the open grandstand.

We all sit down and wait for the race. "This You

Bastard better be good," the cop announces, but no one listens. You can cut the air with a knife, as the trainers, gamblers, thieves, bookies, fat guys, fat girls, chain-smokers, alcos, corrupt cops, and juvenile delinquents all wait, with their scattered thoughts scattering on to the track.

"It *does* look like a rat," I say, when the greyhound we've chosen trots ferret-like and scrawny past us. "And what the hell are clappers, anyway?"

"I don't know," the cop says.

Rube: "We don't know what they are, but we know they're fast."

"Yeah."

The cop and Rube are inseparable now. Best mates. One has a uniform and black, close-cropped hair. The other is in rags, stinks of sweat and No-Name cologne, and has wavy brown-blond hair that staggers toward his shoulders. He has eyes of stomped-out fire, a wet nose that sniffs, and he has bitten claws for fingernails. Needless to say, the second one is my brother. A Wolfe, a dog, through and through.

Then there's the female cop.

Then there's me.

Drooling.

"And they're off!"

It's some tosser, dare I say it, over the loudspeaker, and he's rattling off names of the dogs so fast, I can barely understand him. There's Chewy on a Boot, Dictionary, No Loot, Vicious, and Generic Hound, and they're all in front of You Bastard, who scampers around the back like a rodent with a mousetrap stuck to his arse.

The crowd rises.

They shout.

The female cop looks great.

People scream.

"Go Pictionary! Go Pictionary!"

People correct. "It's *Dic*tionary!"

"What?"

"*Dic*tionary!"

"Oh . . . go *Pic*tionary!"

"Ah, forget it!"

People clap and shout.

Great, I tell you. Great, she looks. Brunette.

Then, finally, the rat gets rid of the mousetrap and makes some ground.

Rube and the cop get happy.

They scream, almost sing with joy. "Go You Bastard! Go You Bastard!"

All of the dogs chase the ludicrous rabbit around the track and the crowd is like an escaped convict.

Running.

Hoping.

Knowing that the world is catching up.

Hanging.

Hanging on for dear life to this moment of liberation that is so sad that it can only lurk. It's the deception of something real inside something so obviously empty.

Screaming.

"Go Vicious!"

"Go No Loot!"

Rube and the cop: "Go You Bastard! Go You Bastard!"

We're all watching as the rat comes flying around the outside of the track, clipping first place and losing balance to fall back into fourth.

"Oh, you bastard!" Rube winces, and he isn't calling the dog by its name as he pedals like hell to make it back.

He does.

He runs well, our bastard.

Runs into second, which makes Rube look at our ticket and ask the cop a question. He says, "Did you bet each way or on the nose?"

By the look on his face, we can tell that the cop has bet on the nose. All or nothing.

"Well, you're a bit useless then, aren't y' mate?" Rube laughs, and he slaps the cop on the back.

"Yep," the cop says. He isn't a tosser anymore. He's just a guy who forgot about the world for a few moments when some dogs sprinted around a track. His name is Gary, a bit of a Nancy-boy name, but who cares?

We say our good-byes and I dream one last time about Cassy the cop and compare her with other imagined women in the lecherous soul that is my youth.

I think about her all the way home, where the usual Saturday night awaits us:

Our sister going out. Our brother staying in, staying quiet. Dad reading the paper. Mrs. Wolfe, our mother, going to bed early. Rube and me talking briefly across the room before sleep.

"I liked her," I say on our front porch.

"I know." Rube smiles and he opens the door.

"Hey Rube, are you awake?"

"Whatta y' reckon? I've only been in here two lousy minutes."

"It's been longer than that."

"It hasn't."

"It has, y' miserable idiot. And tell me what do you want, ay? Can y' tell me that? Whatta y' want?"

"I want you to switch the light off."

"No way."

"It's only fair — I was in here first and you're closer to the switch."

"So what? I'm older. You should respect your elders and switch the light off yourself."

"What a load of bloody."

"It stays on then."

It stays on for ten minutes, and then, take a guess. It's me who switches it off.

"You suck," I tell him.

"Thank you."

CHAPTER 2

There's a noise at about three a.m. It's Sarah spewing her hole in the bathroom. I get up to check her out, and there she is, wrapped around the bowl, hugging it, cradling it. Soaking into it.

Her hair is thick, like all of us in the Wolfe family, and as I look at her through my burning, itchy eyes, I notice that there's some vomit caught in one of her tough tufts of flowing hair. I get some toilet paper and fish it out, then wet a towel to get rid of it altogether.

"Dad?"

"Dad?"

She throws her head back, to the toilet rim. "Is that you, Dad?" and my sister begins to cry. She gathers composure and pulls me to my knees and concentrates on me. With her hands on my shoulders, she wails almost silently. Wailing: "I'm sorry, Dad. I'm sorry I —"

"It's me," I tell her. "It's Cameron."

"Don't lie," she responds. "Don't lie, Dad," and saliva falls to the skin above her red top, hitting her through the heart. Her jeans cut into her hips, slicing them up. It surprises me that they don't draw blood. Same with her heels. Her shoes leave bite marks in her ankles. My sister.

"Don't lie," she says one more time, so I stop.

I stop lying and say, "Okay Sarah, it's me, Dad. We're puttin' you into bed." And to my surprise, Sarah manages to stand up and limp to her room. I get her shoes off, just in time before they sever her feet.

She mumbles.

Words tumble from her mouth as I sit down on the floor, against her bed.

"I'm sick," she says, "of gettin' shattered." She goes on and on, until slowly, she falls.

Asleep.

A *sleep*, I think. *It'll do her good.*

Her last words are, "Thanks Dad . . . I mean, thanks, Cam." Then her hand trips onto my shoulder. It stays. I smile as slightly as a person can smile when they sit, cold, cramped, and crumpled in his sister's room when she's just come home with alcoholic veins, bones, and breath.

Sitting next to Sarah's bed, I think about what's happening with her. I wonder why she's doing this to herself. *Is she lonely?* I ask. *Unhappy? Afraid?* It would be nice if I could say I understand, but that would not be right. No, it wouldn't be, because I just don't know. It would be like asking why Rube and I go down to the dog track. It's not because we're ill-adjusted or we don't fit in or anything like that. It just is. We go to the track. Sarah's getting drunk. She did have a boyfriend once, but he went.

Stop, I tell myself. *Stop thinking about that.* But somehow I can't. Even when I try to think of other things, I just get on to thinking about the other members of my family.

Dad the plumber, who had an accident at work a few months ago and lost all of his jobs. Sure, insurance paid for his injuries, but now he's just plain out of work from it.

Mrs. Wolfe — working hard cleaning people's houses and just got a new job at the hospital.

Steve — working and waiting and dying to leave home.

Then Rube and me — the juveniles.

"Cam?"

Sarah's voice swims to me on a stream of bourbon, Coke, and some other cocktail that drowns the room.

"Cam."

"Cam'ron."

Then sleep.

Then Rube.

He arrives and mutters out a "Huh."

"Can y' flush the toilet?" I ask him. He does it. I hear it, rising and falling like the blowhole down south.

At six, I get up and return to Rube's and my room.

I could kiss Sarah's cheek as I leave, but I don't. Instead, I trounce my hair with my hand, giving up on it in the end — it's bound to stick up. In all directions.

When I get up for real, around seven o'clock, I check on Sarah one last time, just to make sure she hasn't made herself a superstar and choked on her own vomit. She hasn't, but her room's a shocker. The smell is of:

Juice.

Smoke.

Hangover.

And Sarah lying there, caked in it.

Daylight shoots through her window.

I walk.

Out.

Sunday.

I get breakfast, wearing trackies and a T-shirt. I'm barefoot. I watch the end of *Rage* with the volume turned completely down. Then there's a business show that wears a suit and tie and a fake hankie in its pocket.

"Cam."

It's Steve.

"Steve," I nod, and that's about all we'll say to each other for the entire day. Saying each other's name is the way he and I say hello. He always leaves the house early, including on Sundays. He's here but he's not. He'll go to see his friends or go fishing or just disappear. He'll leave the city if he wants. Go down south, where the water's clean and a person passing by will acknowledge you. Not that Steve cares about being acknowledged. He works, he waits. That's all. That's Steve. He offers Mum and Dad to pay more than his board so they can stay ahead, but they won't take it.

Too proud.

Too stubborn.

Dad says we'll manage and that some work is just around the corner. But the corner never ends. It stretches and continues, and Mum drives herself into the ground.

"Thanks."

The day echoes past and that's what Sarah says to me in the evening when I finally see her again. She comes into the lounge room just before dinner.

"I mean it," she tells me softly, and there is something in her eyes that makes me think of *The Old Man and the Sea*, and how the old man's patched sail looks like the flag of permanent defeat. That's what Sarah's eyes look like. The color of defeat chokes her pupils, even though her nod and smile and uncomfortable sitting motion on the couch indicate that she is not finished yet. She will just carry on, like all of us.

Smile stubborn.

Smile with instinct, then lick your wounds in the darkest of dark corners. Trace the scars back to your own fingers and remember them.

At dinner, Rube comes in late, just before Steve.

This is how the Wolfe family looks at the table:

Our mother, eating politely.

Dad, feeding burnt sausage into his mouth but tasting unemployment. His face has healed from the busted pipe that smashed his jaw and ripped open his face. Yes, the injury has healed nicely, at least on the outside of his skin.

Sarah, concentrating on keeping it all down.

Me, watching everyone else.

Rube, swallowing more and more and smiling at something, even though we have an extra dirty piece of business to cater for very soon.

It's Dad who brings it into the foreground.

"Well?" he says when we're done. He looks at Rube and me.

Well what?

"Well what?" Rube asks, but both of us know what we have to do. It's just, we've got an agreement with one of our neighbors that we'll walk his dog for him, twice a week. Sundays and Wednesdays. Let's just say that most of our neighbors think that Rube and me are kind of hoodlums. So to get in the good graces of Keith, the neighbor on our left (who we disturb the most), it was decided that we would walk his dog for him, since he doesn't get much time to do it himself. It was our mother's idea, of course, and we complied. We're many things, Rube and me, but I don't think we're difficult or lazy.

So as the ritual goes, Rube and I grab our jackets and walk out.

The catch is, the dog's a fluffy midget thing called Miffy. Bloody Miffy, for God's sake. What a name. He's a Pomeranian and he's a dead-set embarrassment to walk. So we wait till it gets dark. Then we go next door and Rube hits the highest note in his voice and calls, "Oh Miffy! Miffy!" He grins. "Come to Uncle Rube," and the fluffy embarrassment machine comes prancing toward us like a damned ballerina. I promise you when we're walking that dog and see someone we know, we pull our hoods over our heads and look the other way. I mean, there's only so much guys like us can get away with. Walking a Pomeranian that goes by the name of Miffy is not one of them. Think about it. There's street. Rubbish. Traffic. People yelling at each other over the top of their TVs. Heavy metallers and gang-looking guys slouching past . . . and then there are these two juvenile idiots walking a ball of fluff down the road.

It's out of hand.

That's what it is.

Disgraceful.

"A dis-grace," says Rube.

Even tonight, when Miffy's in a good mood.

Miffy.

Miffy.

The more I say it to myself the more it makes me laugh. The Pomeranian from hell. Watch out, or Miffy'll get you. Well, he's got us all right.

We go out.

We walk him.

We discuss it.

"Slaves are what we are, mate," is Rube's conclusion. We stop. Look at the dog. Carry on. "Look at us. You, me, an' Miffy here, and . . ." His voice trails off.

"What?"

"Nothin'."

"What?"

He gives in easily, because he wanted to all along.

25

At our gate upon our return, Rube looks me in the eye and says, "I was talkin' to my mate Jeff today and he reckons people're talkin' about Sarah."

"Sayin' what?"

"Sayin' she's been gettin' round. Gettin' drunk and gettin' around a bit."

Did he just say what I thought he said?

Getting around?

He did.

He did, and soon, it will alter the life of my brother Rube. It will put him in a boxing ring.

It'll make a heap of girls notice him.

It'll make him successful.

It will drag me with him, and all it will take to start it all is one incident. It's an incident in which he beats the hell out of a guy in school who calls Sarah something pretty ordinary.

For now, though, we stand at our gate.

Rube, Miffy, and me.

"We're wolves," is the last piece of conversation. "Wolves are up higher on the ladder for sure. They oughta *eat* Pomeranians, not walk 'em."

Yet, we do.

Never agree to walk your neighbor's midget dog. Take my word for it.

You'll be sorry.

"Hey Rube."

"What? The light's off this time."

"You reckon it's true what people are sayin'?"

"Reckon what's true?"

"You know — about Sarah."

"I d'know. But if I hear someone sayin' anything about her, I'm gonna nail 'em. I'm gonna kill 'em."

"Y' think so?"

"I wouldn't say it otherwise."

And sure enough, he nearly does.

CHAPTER 3

Rube smashes the guy, with bloody fists and trampling eyes, but first, this:

Our dad's been out of work now for nearly five months. I realize that I've mentioned it before, but I should really explain exactly how it came to be. What happened is that he was working on a site out in the suburbs, when some guy turned on the water pressure too early. A pipe busted and my dad caught the shrapnel, flush in the face.

Busted head.

Broken jaw.

Lots of stitches.

Plenty of wires.

Sure, he's like all fathers, my dad. My old man.

He's okay.

He's hard.

He's sadistic-like. That is, if he's in the mood. Generally though, he's just a human guy with a dog's last name and I feel for him at the moment. He's half a man, because it seems that when a man can't work and when his wife and kids earn all the money, a man becomes half a man. It's just the way it is. Hands grow pale. Heartbeat gets stale.

One thing I must say again, though, is that Dad wouldn't allow Steve or even Sarah to pay a single bill. Just their usual board. Even as he says his regular "No, no, it's okay," you can see where he's been ripped apart. You can see where the shadow opens the flesh and grabs his spirit by the throat. Often, I remember working with him on Saturdays. He'd tell me off and swear when I screwed something up, but he would tell me I did something decently as well. It would be short, to the point.

We are working people.

Work.

Struggle.

Even laugh about it sometimes.

None of us are winners.

We're survivors.

We are wolves, which are wild dogs, and this is our place in the city. We are small and our house is small on our small urban street. We can see the city and the train line and it's beautiful in its own dangerous way. Dangerous because it's shared and taken and fought for.

That's the best way I can put it, and thinking about it, when I walk past the tiny houses on our street, I wonder about the stories inside them. I wonder hard, because houses must have walls and rooftops for a reason. My only query is the windows. Why do they have windows? Is it to let a glimpse of the world in? Or for us to see out? Our own place is small perhaps, but when your old man is eaten by his own shadow, you realize that maybe in every house, something so savage and sad and brilliant is standing up, without the world even seeing it.

Maybe that's what these pages of words are about.

Bringing the world to the window.

"It's okay," Mum says one night. I hear her from my bed as she and Dad discuss paying the bills. I can picture them at the kitchen table, because many things are fought, won, and lost in the kitchen at our place.

Dad replies, "I don't understand it — I used to have

three months' work ahead of me, but since . . ." His voice trails off. I imagine his feet, his jeaned legs, and the scar that angles down the side of his face and onto his throat. His fingers hold each other gently, entwining, making a single fist against the table.

He's wounded.

He's desperate — which makes his next move pretty understandable, even if it can't be condoned.

It's door to door.

Door to dead-set door.

"Well, I've tried advertising in the papers." He raises his voice in the kitchen again. It's the next Saturday. "I've tried everything, so I decided to knock on doors and work cheap. Fix what needs fixin'." While my mother places a chipped mug of coffee in front of him. All she does is stand there, and it's Rube, Sarah, and me that watch.

The next weekend it gets worse, because Rube and I actually see him. We see him as he returns from someone's front gate and we can tell he's copped another rejection. It's strange. Strange to look at him, when just a matter of months ago our father was tough and hard and wouldn't give us an inch. (Not that he does now.

It's just a different feeling, that's all.) He was brutal in his fairness. Cruel in his judgments. Harder than necessary for our own good. He had dirty hands and cash in his pocket and sweat in his armpits.

Rube reminds me of something as we stand there by the street, making sure we don't let him see us.

He says, "Remember when we was kids?"

"*Were* kids."

"Shut up, will y'?"

"Okay."

We walk to a trashed, scabby shop on Elizabeth Street that closed down years ago. Rube continues to talk. It's gray sky again, with blue holes shot through the cloud-blankets. We sit, against a wall, under a bolted-up window.

Rube says, "I remember when we were younger and Dad built a new fence, because the old one was collapsing. I was about ten and you were nine, and the old man was out in the yard, from first light to sunset." Rube brings his knees up to his throat. His jeans cushion his chin, and the bullet holes in the sky widen. I look through them, at what Rube speaks of.

I remember that time quite clearly — how at the end

of a day, when sun was melting back into horizon, Dad turned to us with some nails in his hand and said, "Fellas, these nails here are magic. They're magic nails." And the next day, we woke to the sound of a pounding hammer and we believed it. We *believed* those nails were magic, and maybe they still are now, because they take us back, to that sound. That pounding sound. They take us back to our father as he was: a vision of tall, bent-over strength, with a tough, hard smile and wire-curly hair. There was the slight stoop of his shoulders and his dirty shirt. Eyes of height . . . There was a contentment to him — an air of control, of all-rightness that sat down and hammered in the wake of a tangerine sky, or in that gradual twilight of slight rain, when water fell like tiny splinters from the clouds. He was our father then, not a human.

"Now he's," I answer Rube, "just too real, y' know?" Not much else to say when you've just seen the man knock on doors.

Real.

Reel from it.

Half a man, but.

Still human.

"The bastard," Rube laughs, and I laugh with him, as it seems like the only logical thing to do. "We're gonna cop a hidin' for this at school, ay."

"You're right."

You must understand that we know he's doing his door-knocking in our own district, which means people in school are getting closer and closer to whipping us with remarks. They'll find out all right, and Rube and I will go down heavily. It's just the way it is.

Dad, doors, shame, and in the meantime, Sarah has been out late again.

Three nights.

Three drunken hazes.

Two throw-ups.

Then it happens.

At school.

"Hey Wolfe. Wolfe!"

"What?"

"Your old man came knockin' at our door on the weekend, lookin' for work. Me mum told him he's too useless to even let him *near* our pipes."

Rube laughs.

"Hey Wolfe, I can get your dad a paper run if you want. He could use the pocket money, ay."

Rube smiles.

"Hey Wolfe, when's your old man gonna get the dole?"

Rube stares.

"Hey Wolfe, you might have to leave school and get a job, boy. Y' family could use the extra money."

Rube rubs his teeth together.

Then.

It happens.

The one comment that does it:

"Hey Wolfe, if your family needs the money so bad, your sister should take up whoring. She gets around a bit anyway, I hear. . . ."

Rube.

Rube.

"Rube!" I shout, running.

Too late.

Far too late, because Rube has the guy.

His fingers get bloody from the guy's teeth. His fist hacks through him. Left hand only at first, but it's over and the guy doesn't have a chance. Hardly anyone sees it. Hardly anyone knows, but Rube is standing there. Punches fall fast from his shoulder and land on the guy's face. When they hit him, they pull him apart. They spread out. His legs buckle. He falls. He hits the concrete.

Rube stands and his eyes tread all over the guy.

I stand next to him.

He speaks.

"I don't like this guy very much." A sigh. "He won't get back up. Not in a hurry." He's standing in the guy's eyes, and the last thing he says is, "No one calls my sister a prostitute, slut, whore, or anything else you please to call it." His hair is lifted by the wind, and sun reflects from his face. His tough, scrawny frame is growing good hard flesh by the second, and he smiles. A handful of people have seen what has happened now, and the word is beginning to travel.

More people show up.

"Who?" they ask. "Ruben Wolfe? But he's just a —"

A *what?* I wonder.

"I didn't mean to hit him so hard," Rube mentions, and he sucks on his knuckles. "Or that good." I don't know about him, but I get a flashback of the many fights Rube and I have had in our backyard, with just the one boxing glove each. (You do that when you have only one pair of gloves.)

This time it's different.

This time it's real.

"This time I used both hands," Rube smiles, and I know that we've been thinking about the same thing. I wonder how it feels to really hit someone, to make that final commitment of putting your bare fist in his face, for real. Not just some brotherly thing you do in the backyard, for fun, with boxing gloves.

At home that night, we ask Sarah what's been happening.

She says she's done a few stupid things lately.

We ask her to stop.

She says nothing, but gives us a silent nod.

I keep meaning to ask Rube what it was like to really beat the hell out of that guy, but I never do. I always pull out.

Also, in case you're interested, something has started to stink in our room, but we don't know what it is.

"What the hell *is* that?" Rube asks me. A threatening tone. "Is it y' feet?"

"No."

"Y' socks?"

"No way."

"Y' shoes? Undies?"

"It's this conversation," I suggest.

"Now don't get smart."

"All right!"

"Or I'll crush y'."

"All right."

"Y' little —"

"All *right*!"

"Somethin' always stinks in here," interrupts my dad, who has stuck his head into the room. He shakes his head in amazement, and I feel like everything's going to be okay. Or at least half okay anyway.

"Hey Rube."

"You just woke me, you bastard."

"Sorry."

"No, you're not."

"Yeah, you're right. I'm glad I did. You de-serve it."

"What is it this time?"

"Can't y' hear 'em?"

"Who?"

"Mum and Dad. They're talkin' again in the kitchen. About the bills and all that."

"Yeah. They can't pay 'em too good."

"It's —"

"Bloody hell! What is that smell? It's a dis-grace, ay. Are you sure it's not y' socks?"

"Yes. I'm sure."

I stop and breathe.

I think a question and speak it. Finally.

"Did it feel good to smash that guy?"

Rube: "A little, but not really."

"Why not?"

"Because..." He thinks for a moment. "I

knew I'd beat him and I didn't care about him one bit. I cared about Sarah." I sense him staring at the ceiling. "See, Cameron. The only things I care about in this life are me, you, Mum, Dad, Steve, and Sarah. And maybe Miffy. The rest of the world means nothing to me. The rest of the world can rot."

"Am I like that too?"

"You? No way." There's a slight gap in his words. "And that's your problem. You care about everything."

He's right.

I do.

CHAPTER 4

Mum's cooking pea soup now. It'll last us about a week, which is okay. I can think of worse meals.

"Top-notch soup," Rube tells her after it's swallowed on Wednesday night. Miffy night.

"Well, there's more where that came from," Mum answers.

"Yeah," Rube laughs, and everyone else is pretty quiet.

Steve and Dad have just argued about Dad going on the dole. The silence is slippery. It's dangerous, as I go over what was said:

"I won't do it."

"Why not?"

"Because it's below my dignity."

"Like hell it is. You're even knockin' on doors like a pathetic Boy Scout offering vacuuming and dusting for fifty cents apiece." Steve glares. "And it'd be nice to pay

41

our bills on time," which is when Dad's fist comes down on the table.

"No," and that's pretty much it.

Know that my father will not be bent easily. He will die fighting if he has to.

Steve tries a different tactic. "Mum?"

"No," is her response, and now it's final for sure.

No dole.

No deal.

I feel like saying something about it when we walk Miffy later on, but Rube and I are concentrating too hard on not being noticed by anyone to say anything. Even later, there is no conversation in our room. We both sleep hard and wake up without knowing that this is Rube's day — the day that will change everything. Short and sweet.

It's after school.

It waits.

Outside our front gate.

"Can we talk inside?" a rough bloke asks us. He leans on the gate, not realizing it could fall apart any minute (although he doesn't seem like the type of guy who would care). He is unshaven and wears a jeans jacket.

He has a tattoo on his hand. He puts the question to us again, with just a "Well?"

Rube and I stare.

At him.

At each other.

"Well, for starters," Rube says in the windy street, "who the hell are y'?"

"Oh, I'm sorry," says the guy in his thick city accent. "I'm a guy who can either change your life or smack it into the ground for bein' smart."

We decide to listen.

Needless to say it.

He continues with, "I've heard a rumor that you can fight." He is motioning to Rube. "I have sources at my disposal that never lie, and they say that you gave someone a good caning."

"So?"

Straight to the point now. "So I want you to fight for me. Fifty dollars for a win. A decent tip for a loss."

"I think you'd better come inside."

Rube knows.

This could be interesting.

No one else is home so we sit at the kitchen table and

I make the guy coffee even though he says he wants a beer. Even if we did have beer, I wouldn't give it to this guy. He's arrogant. He's abrasive, and worst of all, he's likable, which always makes a guy difficult to deal with. See, when someone's strictly an awful person, they're easy to get rid of. It's when they make you like them as well that they're hard to contain. Throw likable in and anything can happen. It's a lethal combination.

"Perry Cole."

That's his name. It sounds familiar, but I shrug it off.

"Ruben Wolfe," says Rube. He points at me. "Cameron Wolfe." Both Rube and I shake hands with Perry Cole. The tatt is of a hawk. Real original.

One thing about the guy is that he doesn't muck around. He talks to you and he isn't afraid to lean close, even if his coffee breath reeks like hell. He explains everything straight out. He talks of steady violence, organized fights, raids from police, and everything else that his business involves.

"See," he explains with that succinct, violent voice of his, "I'm part of an organized boxing racket. All through winter, we have fights every Sunday afternoon at four different places in the city. One's a warehouse out the back of Glebe, which is my home arena. One's a meat factory over at Maroubra. One's a warehouse in Ashfield, and there's a pretty decent ring way down south on some guy's farm at Helensburgh." When he speaks, spit fires from his tongue and sticks to the corner of his mouth. "Like I said — you get fifty dollars if you win a fight. You might get a tip if y' lose. People pay in like you wouldn't believe. I mean, you'd think they'd have better things to do on a Sunday afternoon and evening, but they don't. They're sick of football and all that other garbage. They pay five bucks to get in and see up to six fights into the night. Five rounds each and we've had some good fights. We're a few weeks into this season, but I reckon I've got room for you. . . . If you feel like going to one of the other guys who run a team, you'll get the same deal. If you fight well, we'll give you enough money to scrape by, and I myself get rich off the way you fight. That's how it is. You wanna do it?"

Rube hasn't shaved today so he rubs his spiky beard, in thought. "Well, how the hell do I get to all the fights? How'm I gonna get back from Helensburgh on a Sunday night?"

"I've got a van." Easy. "I got a van and I cram all my

fighters in. If you get hurt, I don't take you to a doctor. That's not in the service. If you get killed, your family buries you, not me."

"Ah, stop bein' a tosser," Rube tells him, and all laugh, especially Perry. He likes Rube. I can tell. People like someone who says what they think. "If you die . . ." My brother imitates him.

"One guy came close once," Perry assures him, "but it was a warmer than usual night. It was heat exhaustion and it was only a mild stroke. A heavyweight."

"Oh."

"So," Perry smiles. "You want in?"

"I d'know. I've gotta discuss it with my management."

"Who's your management?" Perry smiles and motions to me with a nod. "It's not this little pansy here, is it?"

"He ain't no pansy." Rube points a finger at him. "He's a cream puff." Then he gets serious. "Actually, he might be a bit skinny, but he can stand up all right, I tell you," which shocks me. Ruben L. Wolfe, my brother, is sticking up for me.

"Is that right?"

"It is. . . . You can check us out if you want. We'll just have us a game of One Punch in the backyard." He looks to me. "We'll just climb over and get Miffy so he doesn't start barking. He likes watching when he's in our yard, doesn't he?"

"He loves it." I can only agree. It's being on the other side of the fence that offends old Miffy. He's gotta be closer to the action, where he can see what's going on. That's when everything's apples. He either watches contentedly or gets bored and goes to sleep.

"Who the hell's Miffy?" Perry asks, confused.

"You'll see."

Rube, Perry, and I stand up and proceed to the back-yard. We put the gloves on, Rube climbs the fence and hands Miffy to me over the top, and One Punch is about to happen. By the look on Perry's face, I can tell he'll appreciate it.

We each wear our solitary boxing glove, but Miffy the Pomeranian is demanding attention and pats. We both crouch down and pat the midget dog. Perry watches. He looks like the kind of guy who would drop-kick a dog like this from here to eternity. As it turns out, he isn't.

"The dog's an embarrassment," Rube explains to him, "but we have to look out for 'im."

"Come 'ere, fella." Perry holds out his fingers for the

dog to sniff and Miffy likes him immediately. He sits next to him as Rube and I start our game of One Punch.

Perry loves it.

He laughs.

He smiles.

He watches with curiosity when I hit the ground the first time.

He pats Miffy happily when I hit it the second time.

He claps when I get Rube a good one on the jaw. Just a good, solid clip.

After fifteen minutes we stop.

Rube says, "I told you, didn't I?" and Perry nods.

"Show us a bit more," he states calmly, "but swap gloves." He looks like he's thinking hard. Then he watches as Rube and I go at it again.

It's tougher with the other glove. We both miss more, but slowly, we get into a rhythm. We circle the yard. Rube throws out his hand. I duck it. Swerve. Make my way in. I jab. Hit his chin. Shoot one at his ribs. He counterpunches. His breath is stern as he stabs his fist through my cheekbone, then gets me in the throat.

"Sorry."

"Okay."

We resume.

He gets one under my ribs and I can't breathe. A yelp escapes from under my breath.

Rube stands.

So do I, but crooked.

"Finish him off," Perry tells him.

Rube does it.

When I wake up, the first thing I see is Miffy's dog-ugly face pressed into mine. Then I see Perry, smiling. Then I see Rube, worried.

"I'm okay," I tell him.

"Good."

When they get me back up, we all walk back into the kitchen and Rube and Perry sit down. I slump down. I feel like death warmed up. A strip of green flanks my vision. Static reaches through my ears.

Perry motions to the fridge. "Y' sure you don't have a beer?"

"Are you an alcoholic or somethin'?"

"I just like a beer now and then."

"Well." Rube is forthright. "We don't have one." He's a bit upset about knocking me unconscious, I can tell. I remember him saying, *The only things I care about in this life . . .*

Perry decides to get back down to business.

What he says is a shock.

It's this:

"I want both of y's."

Rube sniffs, with surprise, and rubs his nose.

Perry looks now at Rube and says, "You . . ." He smiles. "You can fight, all right. That's a fact." Then he looks at me. "And you've got heart. . . . See, one thing I didn't go into detail about before was the tips. People throw money into the ring corners if they think you've got heart, and . . . it's Cameron, isn't it?"

"Yeah."

"Well, you've got it in spades."

Trying not to, I smile. Damn guys like Perry. You hate them, but they still make you smile.

"So what will happen is this." He looks at Rube. "You're gonna win fights and you'll be popular because you're fast and young and you've got a rough but some-how attractive head."

I look at my brother now as well. I examine him, and it's true. He *is* good-looking, but in a strange way. It's sudden, rough, rugged. A wayward kind of handsome that's more around him than on him. It's more of a feeling, or an aura.

Perry looks now at me. "And you? You'll most likely get hammered, but if you keep clean enough and stay off the ropes, you'll get close to twenty bucks in tips, 'cause people will see your heart."

"Thanks."

"No need for thanking. These are facts." No more time-wasting. "So do you want in or not?"

"I don't know about my brother," Rube admits to him, with caution. "He can take a beating in the backyard, but that's different to taking it week in week out by some guy who wants to kill him."

"He'll fight someone new each week."

"So what?"

"Most of 'em are good fighters but some are dead average. They're just desperate for the money." He shrugs. "Y' never know. The kid might win a few."

"What are the other dangers?"

"In general?"

"Yes."

"They're these." He makes the list. "Rough guys

watch the fights and if you back out of a bout they might kill y'. Some nice girls come along with these guys and if you touch 'em those guys might kill y'. Last year, some cops were getting close to raiding an old factory we were using in Petersham. If they catch y', they'll kill y'. So if that happens, run." He's pretty happy with himself, especially for the last one: "The biggest danger, though, is leaving *me* in the lurch. If you do it, *I'll* kill y', and that's worse than all the others put together."

"Fair enough."

"You wanna think about it?"

"Yeah."

To me: "How 'bout you?"

"Me too."

"Right," and he stands up, handing us his phone number. It's written on a piece of torn cardboard. "You've got four days. Ring me on Monday night at seven sharp. I'll be home."

Rube has two more questions.

The first: "What if we join and then wanna quit?"

"Up until August, you have to give me two weeks' notice or find someone to take your place. That's all. People quit all the time because it's a rough game. I understand. Just two weeks' notice or three legitimate names of blokes that can fight well. They're everywhere. No one's irreplaceable. If you make it to August, you've gotta finish the season, into September, when the semifinals are on. See, we do a draw, a competition ladder, the lot. We have finals and everything, with more money in 'em."

The second question: "What weight divisions will we fight in?"

"You'll both be in lightweight."

This triggers a question in me.

"Will we ever fight each other?"

"Maybe, but the chance is pretty slight. Once in a while, fighters from the same team have to fight each other. It does happen. You got a problem with that?"

"Not really." It's Rube who says it.

"Me neither."

"Well why'd y' ask?"

"Just curious."

"Any more questions?"

We think.

"No."

"Good," and we see Perry Cole out of our house. On

the front porch, he reminds us. "Remember, you've got four days. Ring me Monday night at seven with yes or no. I'll be unhappy if you don't ring — and I'm not someone you want unhappy with you."

"All right."

He leaves.

We watch him get into his car. It's an old Holden, done up well, and it must be worth a bit. He must be rolling in money to have both his van *and* this car. It's money earned off desperates like us.

Once back inside, we hang around with Miffy, feeding him some bacon fat. Nothing. Not yet. Miffy just rolls around and we pat his stomach. I go to our room to try and find out once and for all what stinks in there. It's not going to be pretty.

"Yes, I'm awake."

"How'd y' know I was gonna ask?"

"You always do."

"I found out what the smell was."

"And?"

"Remember when we got that job lot of onions from the fruit shop?"

"What? The ones my mates stole? Last Christmas?"

"Yeah."

"That was six bloody months ago!"

"A few strays must have got out of the bag. They were under my bed, in the corner, all disgusting and rotten."

"Oh, man."

"Damn right. I chucked 'em in the compost, up near the back fence."

"Good idea."

"I was gonna show 'em to y', but they stank so bad, I fully ran out there with 'em."

"Even better idea... Where was I?"

"Next door, returnin' Miffy."

"Oh yeah."

Change of topic.

"Are y' thinkin' about it?" I ask. "About that Perry character?"

"Yep."

"You reckon we can do it?"

"Hard to say."

"It sounds . . ."

"What?"

"I d'know — scary."

"It's a chance."

. . . Yes, but a chance at what, I wonder. Our bedroom seems extra dark tonight. Heavy dark.

I think it again. A chance at what?

CHAPTER 5

t's Friday evening and we're watching *Wheel of Fortune*. It's rare for us to watch a lot of TV because we're usually fighting, doing something stupid in the backyard, or hanging around out front. Besides, we hate most of the crap on the telly anyway. The only good thing about it is that sometimes when you watch it, you can get a bright idea. Previous bright ideas we've had in the midst of TV are:

Attempting to rob a dentist.

Moving the small lounge table up onto the couch so we could play football against each other with a rolled-up pair of socks.

Going to the dog track for the first time.

Selling Sarah's busted old hair-dryer to one of our neighbors for fifteen dollars.

Selling Rube's broken tape player to a guy down the street.

Selling the telly.

Obviously, we could never carry out *all* of the good ideas.

The dentist was a disaster (we pulled out, of course). Playing football with the socks resulted in giving Sarah a fat lip when she walked through the lounge room. (I swear it was Rube's elbow and not mine that hit her.) The dog track was fun (even though we came back twelve bucks poorer than when we left). The hair-dryer was thrown back over the fence with a note attached that said, *Give us back our fifteen bucks or we'll bloody kill you, you cheating bastards.* (We gave the money back the next day.) We couldn't end up finding the tape player (and the guy down the street was pretty tight anyway so I doubt we'd have got much for it). Then, last of all, there was just no way we could ever sell the TV, even though I came up with eleven good reasons why we should give the telly the chop. (They go like this:

One. In ninety-nine percent of shows, the good guys win in the end, which just isn't the truth. I mean, let's face it. In real life, the bastards win. They get all the girls, all the cash, all the everything. Two. Whenever there's a sex scene, everything goes perfectly, when really, the people in the shows should be as scared of it as me. Three. There are a thousand ads. Four. The ads are always much louder than the actual shows. Five. The news is always kind of depressing. Six. The people are all beautiful. Seven. All the best shows get the ax. For example, *Northern Exposure*. Have you heard of it? No? Exactly — it got the ax years ago. Eight. Rich blokes own all the stations. Nine. The rich blokes own beautiful women as well. Ten. The reception can be a bit of a shocker at our place anyway because our aerial's shot. Eleven. They keep showing repeats of a show called *Gladiators*.)

The only question now is, *What's today's idea?* The truth is, it's more of a decision to conclude on last night, as Rube speaks over at me. He starts with an "Oi."

"Oi," he says.

"Yeah?"

"What are your thoughts?"

"On what?"

"You know what. Perry."

"We need the money."

"I know, but Mum and Dad won't let us help pay the bills."

"Yeah, but we can hold our own end up — pay our own food and stuff so everything lasts longer."

"Yeah, I s'pose."

Then Rube says it.

It's decided.

Concluded.

Ended.

He speaks the words, "We're gonna do it."

"Okay."

Only, we know we won't pay our own food. No. We have no intention. We're doing this for some other reason. Some other reason that wants inside us.

Now we have to wait till Monday so we can ring Perry Cole, but already, we have to think — about everything. About other guys' fists. About the danger. About Mum and Dad finding out. About survival. A new world has arrived in our minds and we have to handle it. We have decided and there is no time to stick our tail between our legs and run. We've decided in front of the telly and that means we have to give it a shot. If we succeed, good. If we fail, it's nothing new.

Rube's thinking about it, I can tell.

Personally, I try not to.

I try to focus on the woman's brilliant legs on *Wheel of Fortune*. When she swivels the letters, I can see more of them, just before she turns around and smiles at me. She smiles pretty, and in that split second, I forget. I forget about Perry Cole and all those future punches. It makes me wonder, *Do we spend most of our days trying to remember or forget things?* Do we spend most of our time running toward or away from our lives? I don't know.

"Who y' goin' for?" Rube interrupts my thoughts, looking at the TV.

"I d' know."

"Well?"

"Okay then." I point. "I'll take the dopey one in the middle."

"That's the host, y' idiot."

"Is it? Well, I'll take the blonde one there on the end. She looks the goods."

"I'll take the guy on the other end. The one who

looks like he just escaped from Long Bay Jail. His suit's a dead-set outrage. It's a dis-grace."

In the end it's the guy from Long Bay that wins. He gets a vacuum cleaner and has already won a trip to the Great Wall of China, from yesterday apparently. Not bad. The trip, that is. In the champion round, he misses out on a ridiculous remote control bed. In all honesty, the only thing keeping us watching is to see the woman turning the letters. I like her legs and so does Rube.

We watch.

We forget.

We know.

We know that on Monday we'll be ringing Perry Cole to tell him we're in.

"We better start training then," I tell Rube.

"I know."

Mum comes home. We don't know where Dad is.

Mum takes the compost out to the heap in the back-yard.

Upon returning she says, "Something really stinks out there near the back fence. Do either of you know anything about it?"

We look at each other. "No."

"Are you sure?"

"Well," I crack under the pressure. "It was a few onions that were in our room that we forgot about. That's all."

Mum isn't surprised. She never is anymore. I think she actually accepts our stupidity as something she just can't change. Yet she still asks the question. "What were they doing in your room?" However, she walks away. I don't think she really wants to hear the answer.

When Dad arrives, we don't ask where he's been.

Steve comes in and gives us a shock by saying, "How y' goin', lads?"

"All right. You?"

"Good." Even though he still watches Dad with contempt, wishing he'd get the dole or Job Search payments or whatever you please to call it. He soon changes clothes and goes out.

Sarah comes in eating a banana Paddlepop. She smiles and gives us both a bite. We don't ask for one, but she knows. She can see our snouts itching for the gorgeous sickly cold of an iceblock in winter.

Next day, Rube and I begin training.

We get up early and run. It's dark when the alarm goes off and we take a minute or two to get out of bed, but once out, we're okay. We run together in track pants and old football jerseys and the city is awake and smoky-cold and our heartbeats jangle through the streets. We're alive. Our footsteps are folded neatly, one after the other. Rube's curly hair collides with sunlight. The light steps at us between the buildings. The train line is fresh and sweet and the grass in Belmore Park has the echoes of dew still on it. Our hands are cold. Our veins are warm. Our throats suck in the winter breath of the city, and I imagine people still in bed, dreaming. To me, it feels good. Good city. Good world, with two wolves running through it, looking for the fresh meat of their lives. Chasing it. Chasing hard, even though they fear it. They run anyway.

"Y' awake, Rube?"

"Yeah."

"Jeez, I'm a bit sore, ay. This runnin' in

the mornings isn't much chop for the ol' legs."

"I know — mine are sore too."

"It felt good but."

"Yeah. It felt great."

"It felt like I'm not sure what. Like we've finally got something. Something to give us — I d'know. I just don't know."

"Purpose."

"What?"

"Purpose," Rube continues. "We've finally got a reason to be here. We've got reason to be out on that street. We're not just out there doin' nothin'."

"That's it. That's exactly how it felt."

"I know."

"But I'm still sore as hell."

"Me too."

"So are we still runnin' again tomorrow?"

"Absolutely."

"Good." And in the darkness of our room, a smile reaches across my lips. I feel it.

CHAPTER 6

"**B**loody hell."

The phone's been cut off because we don't have the money to pay the bill. Or really, Mum and Dad don't have the money to pay it. Steve or Sarah could pay, but there's no way. It's not allowed. It isn't even considered.

"Well, up this, then," Steve rips through the kitchen air. "I'm movin' out. Soon as possible."

"Then they miss y' board money," Sarah tells him.

"So what? If they wanna suffer they can do it without me watchin'." It's fair enough.

As well as being fair enough, it's Monday night, and it's close to seven. This is not good. This is *very* not good. Very not good at all.

"Oh no," I say across to Rube. He's warming his

hands above the toaster. This means we can't use the phone in Sarah's room to ring Perry. "Hey Rube."

"What?" His toast pops up.

"The phone."

He realizes.

He says, "Bloody typical. Is this house useless or what?" and the toast is forgotten.

We go next door with Perry's number in Rube's pocket. No one home.

We go the other side. The same.

So Rube runs into our house, flogs forty cents out of Steve's wallet, and we take off. It's ten to seven. "You know where there's a public phone?" Rube talks between strides. We pant. This is close to a sprint.

"Trust me," I assure him. I know about phone boxes in this district.

I sniff one out and we find it hunched in the darkness of a side street.

It's bang on seven when we ring.

"You're late," are Perry's first words. "I don't like being kept waiting."

"Calm down," Rube tells him. "Our phone got cut

and we just ran close to three Ks to get here. Besides, my watch says seven sharp."

"Okay, okay. Is that y' breathing I can hear?"

"I told you, we just ran nearly."

"All right." Business. "Are you in or out?"

Rube.

Me.

Heartbeat.

Breath.

Heartbeat.

Voice.

"In."

"Both of y's?"

A nod.

"Yeah," Rube states, and we can feel Perry smiling through the phone line.

"Good," he says. "Now listen. Y' first fights won't be this week. They'll be the week after, out at Maroubra. First though, we gotta get some things organized. I'll tell y's what y' need and we've gotta give you some hype. Y' need names. Y' need gloves. We'll talk about it. Can I come over again or do y's wanna meet somewhere else?"

"Central," is Rube's suggestion. "Our old man might be home and that won't be apples."

"Okay. Central it is. Tomorrow, four o'clock. Down at Eddy Avenue, where it leads into Belmore Park."

"Sounds good."

"Good."

It's settled.

"Welcome," is Perry's final word, and the phone runs dead. We're in.

We're in and it's final.

We're in and it's final, because if we back out now, we'll probably end up at the bottom of the harbor. Down near the oil spill, in garbage bags. Well, that's exaggerating, of course, but who knows? Who knows what kind of seedy world we've just entered? Our only knowledge is that we can make money, and maybe some self-respect.

As we walk back, it feels like the city is engulfing us. Adrenaline still pours through our veins. Sparks flow through to our fingers. We've still been running in the mornings, but the city's different then. It's filled with hope and with bristles of winter sunshine. In the evening, it's like it dies, waiting to be born again the next morning. I see a dead starling as we walk. It's next to a beer bottle in the gutter. Both are empty of soul, and we can only walk by in silence, watching people who watch us, ignoring people who ignore us, and Rube growling at people who attempt to force us from the footpath. Our eyes are large and rimmed with awakeness. Our ears detect every opened-up sound. We smell the impact of traffic and humans. Humans and traffic. Back and forth. We taste our moment, swallowing it, knowing it. We feel our nerves twitching inside our stomachs, lunging at our skin from beneath.

When morning slits across the horizon the following day, we have already been running for a while. As we do so, Rube discusses a few things with me. He wants a punching bag. He wants a skipping rope. He wants more speed and another pair of gloves so we can fight properly for practice. He wants headgear so we don't kill each other doing it. He wants.

He wants hard.

He runs and there is purpose in his feet, and there's hunger in his eyes and desire in his voice. I've never seen him like this. Like he wants so savagely to be somebody and to fight for it.

When we get home, sunshine splashes across his face. Again. A collision.

He says, "We're gonna do it, Cam." He is serious and solemn. "We're gonna get there, and for once, we're gonna win. We're not leavin' without winning." He's leaning on the gate. He crouches. He buries his face into the horizontal paling. Fingers in the wire. Then, a shock, because when he turns his head back up to look at me, there's a tear dangling from his eye. It edges down his face and his voice is smothered with his hunger. He says, "We can't accept bein' just us any-more. We've gotta lift. Gotta be more . . . I mean, check Mum out. Killin' herself. Dad down and out. Steve just about moved and gone. Sarah gettin' called a slut." He tightens his fist in the wire and explains it through half-clenched teeth. "So now it's us. It's simple. We've gotta lift. Gotta get our self-bloody-respect back."

"Can we?" I ask.

"We've gotta. We will." He stands and grabs me by the front of my jersey, right at my heart. He says, "I'm Ruben Wolfe," and he says it hard. He throws the words into my face. "And you're Cameron Wolfe. That's gotta start meaning somethin', boy. That's gotta start churnin'

72

inside us, making us wanna be someone for those names, and not be just another couple of guys who amounted to nothin' but what people said we would. No way. We're gettin' out of that. We have to. We're gonna crawl and moan and fight and bite and bark at anything that gets in our way or tries to hunt us down and shoot us. All right?"

"Okay." I nod.

"Good," and to my dismay, Rube leans on my shoulder with his forearm and we stare onto the morning street of black light and glinting cars. I feel that we're together to face whatever falls down around us, and it staggers me for a moment that Rube has grown up (even though he's a year older than me). It staggers me that he wants and aches so hard. His final words are, "If we fail, we're gonna blame *us*."

We walk inside soon after, knowing he's right. The only people we want to blame are ourselves, because it will be ourselves that we rely upon. We're aware of it, and the knowing will always walk beside us, at the edge of each day, on the outskirts of each pulse in each heartbeat. We eat breakfast, but our hunger is not fed. It's growing.

It grows even more when we meet Perry at Eddy Avenue, just like he told us. Four o'clock.

"Lads," he greets us. He carries a small suitcase.

"Perry."

"Hi Perry."

We all walk together to a bench near the middle of the park. The bench has been slapped hard by the pigeons from above, so it's a pretty *dodgy* place to be sitting. Not something you'd eat off. Still, it's safer than some of the others, which the birds seem to recognize as their own public toilets.

"Check the state of this place," Perry smirks. He's the kind of guy who likes to sit in a scummy park and talk business. "It's disgraceful," though his smirk is now a full-blown smile. It's a smile of diseased malice, friendliness, and happiness all rolled into one devastating concoction. He wears a flanno, rough jeans, old boots, and of course, that vicious smile of his. He looks for a place on the table to put the suitcase but settles for the ground.

A pause of silence arrives.

An old man comes to us asking for change.

Perry gives him some, but first he asks the poor old bloke a question.

He says, "Mate, what's the capital of Switzerland, do y' know?"

"Bern," the old man replies, after some thought.

"Very good. However, my point is this." He smiles again. Damn that smile. "In that country, once, they gathered up all the gypsies, whores, and drunken bums such as yourself, and they threw 'em over the border. They got rid of every dirty swine that graced their precious land."

"So?"

"So you're an incredibly lucky drunken bum now, aren't you? You not only get to stay in our fine land, but you also earn a living out of kindhearted people such as myself, and my colleagues here."

"They didn't give me anything."

(We blew our last cash at the dog track the other day.)

"Certainly, but they didn't throw you in the Pacific either now, did they?" He grins, evil. "They didn't chuck you out there and tell you to start swimming." He adds for good measure, "Like they should have."

"You're crazy." The drunk begins to leave.

"Of course I am," Perry calls after him. "I just gave you a dollar of my hard-earned wages."

Yeah, right, I think. *It's money he earns from fighters.* The old man is already on to the next people — a grungy black-dressed couple with purple hair. They've got earrings stapled across their faces, and Docs on their feet.

"He oughta give *them* the buck now," Rube observes, and I laugh. He's about right, and as the old man lingers around the couple, I watch him. He has turned his life into the pocket scraps of other people. It's sad.

It's sad, but Perry has forgotten all about the man. He's had his pleasure and is now strictly onto business.

"Right." He points at me. "We'll get you out of the way first. Here are your gloves and shorts. I thought about shoes but you're not getting any. Neither of you are worth it, because I don't know how long you'll last. I might get you some later, so wear your gymmies for now."

"Fair enough."

I take my gloves and shorts and like them.

They're cheap, but I like them a lot. Blood-colored gloves and navy-blue shorts.

"Now." Perry lights a cigarette and pulls a warm beer from the suitcase. Smokes and beer cans. He annoys me with that garbage, but I listen on. "We need to get you a name, for when you get introduced to the crowd before your fights. Any ideas?"

"The Wolf Man?" Rube suggests.

I shake my head.

Thinking.

It hits me.

Smiling.

I know. I nod. I say it.

"The Underdog."

I continue to smile as Perry's face lights up and I watch old beggars and weirdos and city pigeons scouring the city floor for the sake of their lives.

Yes, Perry lights up, behind his smoke, and says, "Nice. I like it. Everyone loves an underdog. It appeals to them and even if y' lose they'll send some tips your way." A laugh. "It's better than nice. It's flat-out perfect."

No time-wasting though.

"Now," he moves on. There's a finger pointed at Rube. "You're all sorted out. Here are y' gloves an' shorts." Gray-blue gloves. Cheap. No laces. Just like mine. His shorts are black with gold rims. Nicer than mine. "You wanna know what name you've got?"

"Don't I get a choice?"

"No."

"Why not?"

"Y' sorted out, that's why. Tell y' what, you'll find out when you fight, okay?"

"I s'pose."

"Say yes." Forceful.

"Yes."

"And say thank you, because when I'm done with you, the women'll fall over you like dominoes."

Dominoes.

What a tosser.

Rube obeys him. "Thank you."

"Right."

Perry stands and leaves, suitcase by his side.

He turns.

He says, "Let me remind you fellas that your first fight

is next Sunday at Maroubra. I'll take you there in my van. Be here at Eddy Avenue again at three o'clock sharp. Don't make me wait or a bus'll clean me up and I'll clean the pair of *you* up. Okay?"

We nod.

He's gone.

"Thanks for the gear," I call, but Perry Cole is gone.

We sit there.

Gloves.

Shorts.

Park.

City.

Hunger.

Us.

"Damn it."

"What, Rube?"

"It's been annoyin' me all day and night."

"What?"

"I wanted to ask Perry if he could get his

hands on a punching bag for us, and some of that other practice gear."

"You don't need a punching bag."

"Why not?"

"You've got me."

"Yeah."

"Y' didn't have to agree."

"I wanted to."

A long pause ...

"Are y' scared, Rube?"

"No. I was before, but not anymore. Are you?"

"Yeah."

There's no point lying. I'm scared as hell. Scared crazy. I'm asylum scared. Strait-jacket scared. Yes, I think it's pretty much decided.

I'm scared.

CHAPTER 7

Time has elapsed and it's the Sunday morning. Fight day, and I'm dying to get into the bathroom. I have to do a nervous one. We've trained hard. Running, push-ups, sit-ups, the lot. Even skipping, with Miffy's leash. We've done One Punch and also fought two-handed with our new gloves, every afternoon. Rube keeps telling me we're ready, but still, I have to go. Desperately.

"Who's *in* there?" I cry through the door. "I'm in agony out here, ay."

A voice booms back. "It's me." Me as in Dad. Me as in the old man. Me as in the guy who may be unemployed but can still give us a good kick in the pants for being smart. "Give me two minutes."

Two minutes!

How am I going to survive two minutes?

When he finally comes out, I feel like I'm going to collapse onto the seat, but the doorway's as far as I get. *Why's that?* you may well ask, but I tell you, if you're anywhere near our bathroom this morning, you'll be tasting the worst smell you've ever swallowed in your whole life. The smell is twisted. It's angry. No, it's downright ropeable.

I breathe and choke and breathe again, turning around, almost running. Now, though, I'm almost howling with laughter as well.

"What?" Rube asks when I make it back to our room.

"Oh, mate."

"What is it?"

"Come 'ere." I tell him, and we walk back toward the bathroom.

The smell hits me again.

It smacks into Rube.

"Whoa." That's all he says, at first.

"Shockin', ay?" I ask.

"Well, it isn't too cheerful, is it, that smell," Rube admits. "What's the old man been eating lately?"

"I've got no idea," I go on, "but I'm tellin' y' right now — that smell's physical."

"Damn right." Rube backs away from it. "It's bloody relentless is what it is. Like a gremlin, a monster, a —" He's lost for words.

I muster up some courage and say, "I'm goin' in."

"Why?"

"I'm dyin' here!"

"Okay, good luck."

"I'll need it."

I'll need more later though, and I feel the nerves, waiting at Eddy Avenue. Fingers of fear and doubt scratch the lining of my stomach. I feel like I'm bleeding inside, but it's only nerves. I'm sure. Rube, on the other hand, sits with his legs stretched out. His hands rest firmly on his hips. His face is awash with his hair, blown in from the wind. A small smile is forming on his lips. His mouth opens.

"He's here," my brother says. "Let's go."

The van pulls in — a real heap of a thing. A Kombi. Four other guys are already in it. We enter it, through the sliding door.

"Glad y's could make it." Perry grins at us through the rear vision mirror. He's wearing a suit today. Bloodred and tough to look at. It's nice.

"I had to cancel my violin recital," Rube tells him, "but we made it." He sits down and some guy the size of an outhouse slides the door shut. His name is Bumper. The lean guy next to him is Leaf. The fatty sort of bloke is Erroll and the normal-looking one is Ben. They're all older than us. Daunting. Scarred. Fist-weathered.

"Rube 'n' Cameron." Perry introduces us, via the mirror again.

"Hey."

Silence.

Violent eyes.

Broken noses.

Missing teeth.

In my uneasiness, I look to Rube. He doesn't ignore me, but rather, he closes a fist as if to say, "Stay awake."

Minutes follow.

They're silent minutes. Awake. Moving. On edge, as I concentrate on survival, and hope for this trip to never end. Hope to never get there. . . .

We pull into the meat factory out the back of Maroubra and it's cold and windy and salty.

People hang.

Around us, I can sniff out a savagery in the noisy southern air. It knifes its way into my nose, but I do not bleed blood. It's fear I bleed, and it gushes out over my lip. I wipe it away, in a hurry.

"C'mon." Rube drags me with him. "This way boy, or do y' wanna play with the locals?"

"No way."

Inside, Perry takes us through a small room and into a freezing compartment, where some dead frozen pigs hang like martyrs from the ceiling. It's terrible. I stare at them a moment, with the tightened air and the frightening sight of dead cut meat gouging at my throat.

"It's just like Balboa," I whisper to Rube. "The hangin' meat."

"Yeah," he replies. He knows what I mean.

It makes me wonder what we're doing here. All the other fellas just wait around, even sit, and they smoke, or they drink alcoholic beverages to eat the nerves. To calm the fear. To slow the fists but quicken the courage.

That huge bloke, Bumper, he winks at me, enjoying my fear.

He's just sitting there and his quiet voice comes to me, casually.

"The first fight's the toughest." A smile. "Don't worry about winning it. Survive first, then consider it. Okay?"

I nod, but it's Rube who speaks.

He speaks, "Don't worry, mate. My brother knows how to get up."

"Good." He means it. Then, "How 'bout you?"

"Me?" Rube smiles. He's tough and sure and doesn't seem to have any fear. Or at least he won't show it. He only says, "I won't need to get up," and the thing is, he knows he won't. Bumper knows he won't. *I* know he won't. You can smell it on him, like that guy in *Apocalypse Now* that everyone knows won't die. He loves the war too much, and the power. He doesn't even consider death, let alone fear it. And that's exactly how Rube is. He's walking out of here with fifty dollars and a grin. That's it. Nothing more to say about it.

We meet some people.

"So you've got some new blokes, ay?" an ugly old guy smiles at Perry — a smile like a stain. He sums us up and points. "The little one's got no hope, but the older fella looks all right. A bit pretty maybe, but not too bad at all. Can he fight?"

"Yeah," Perry assures him, "and the little one's got heart."

"Good." A scar crawls up and down the old guy's chin. "If he keeps gettin' up, we might just have us a slaughter. We haven't had a slaughter here for weeks." He gets right in my eyes, for power. "We might just hang him up here with the pigs."

"How about you leave, old man?" Rube steps closer. "Or maybe we'll hang you up instead."

The old man.

Rube.

Their eyes are fixed on each other, and the man is dying to have Rube against the wall, I swear it, but something stops him. He only makes a brief statement.

He states, "You all know the rules, lads. Five rounds

or until one of y's can't get up. The crowd's restless tonight. They want some blood, so be careful. I've got me some hard fellas myself, and they're keen, just like you. See you out there."

When he leaves, it's Perry who has Rube up against the wall. He warns him. "If you ever do that again, that guy'll kill you. Understand?"

"Okay."

"Say yes."

Rube smiles. "Okay." A shrug. "Yes."

He releases him and straightens his suit. "Good."

Perry then takes us through another hall and into a new room. Through a crack in the door, we see the crowd. There are at least three hundred of them. Probably more, all crammed into the cleared factory floor.

They drink beer.

They smoke.

They talk.

Smile.

Laugh.

Cough.

It's a crowd of stupid men, old and young. Surfers, footballers, Rednecks, the lot.

They wear jackets and black jeans and rough coats and some of them have women or girls clinging to them. They're brainless girls, otherwise they wouldn't be seen dead here. They're pretty, with ugly, appealing smiles and conversations we can't hear. They breathe smoke and blow it out, and words drop from their mouths and get crushed to the floor. Or they get discarded, just to glow with warmth for a moment, for someone else to tread on later.

Words.

Just words.

Just sticky-blond words, and when I see the ring all lit up and silent, I can imagine those women cheering later on when I hit the canvas floor, my face all bruised up and bloody.

Yes.

They'll cheer, I reckon.

Cigarette in one hand.

Warm, sweaty hand of a thug in the other.

Screaming, blond, beer-filled mouth.

All of that, and a spinning room.

That's what scares me most.

"Hey Rube, what're we doin' here?"

"Shut up."

"I can't believe we got ourselves into this!"

"Stop whisperin'."

"Why?"

"If y' don't, I'll be forced to trounce you myself."

"Really?"

"You're startin' to aggravate me, y' know that?"

"I'm sorry."

"We're ready."

"Are we?"

"Yes. Don't you feel it?"

I ask myself.

Are y' ready Cameron?

Again.

Are y' ready Cameron?

Time will tell.

It's funny, don't you think, how time seems to do a lot of things? It flies, it tells, and worst of all, it runs out.

CHAPTER 8

t's the sound of my breathing that gets me, pouring down into my lungs and then tripping back up my throat. Perry's just come in and told me. It's time.

"You're up first," he says.

It's time and I'm still sitting there, in my old, too-big-for-me spray jacket. (Rube's got an old hooded jacket of Steve's.) All is numb. My hands, fingers, feet. It's time.

I stand up.

I wait.

Perry's gone back out to the ring, and the next time the door opens, I'll be heading there myself. With no more time to think, it happens. The door is opened and I start walking out. Out into.

The arena.

Aggression quivers inside me. Fear shrouds me. Footsteps take me forward.

Then the crowd.

They lift my spirit, as I'm the first fighter to come out.

They turn and look at me in my spray jacket, and I walk through them. The hood is out and over my head. They cheer. They clap and whistle, and this is just the beginning. They howl and chant, and for a moment, they forget the beer. They don't even feel it pouring down their throats. It's just me, and the fact that violence is near. I'm the messenger. I'm the hands and feet. I bring it to them. I deliver it.

"THE UNDERDOG!"

It's Perry, standing in the ring, holding a microphone.

"Yes, it's Cameron Wolfe, the Underdog!" he shouts through the mike. "Give the boy a hand — our youngest fighter! Our youngest battler! Our youngest brawler! He'll fight to the end, people, and he'll keep getting up!"

The hood of the jacket is still over my head, even though it has no string, no anything to hold it in place. My boxing shorts are comfortable on my legs. My gym boots walk on, through the sharp, thick crowd.

They're alert now.

Awake.

Eager.

They watch me and size me up and they're tough and hard and suddenly respectful.

"Underdog," they murmur, all the way to the ring, till I climb in. Rube's behind me. He'll be in my corner, just like I'll sit in his.

"Breathe," I say to me.

I look.

Around.

I walk.

From one side of the ring to the other.

I crouch.

Down in my corner.

When I'm there, Rube's eyes fire into mine. *Make sure you get up*, they tell me, and I nod, then jump up. The jacket's off. My skin's warm. My wolfish hair sticks up as always, nice and thick. I'm ready now. I'm ready to keep standing up, no matter what, I'm ready to believe that I welcome the pain and that I want it so much that I will look for it. I will seek it out. I'll run to it and throw myself into it. I'll stand in front of it in blind terror and let it beat me down and down till my courage hangs off me in rags. Then it will dismantle me and stand me up naked and beat me some more and my

94

slaughter-blood will fly from my mouth and the pain will drink it, feel it, steal it, and conceal it in the pockets of its gut and it will taste me. It will just keep standing me up, and I won't let it know. I won't tell it that I feel it. I won't give it the satisfaction. No, the pain will have to kill me.

That's what I want right now as I stand in the ring, waiting for the doors to open again. I want the pain to kill me before I give in. . . .

"And now!"

I stare into the canvas floor beneath me.

"You know who it is!"

I close my eyes and lean on the ropes with my gloves.

"Yes!" It's the old ugly guy who yells now. "It's Cagey Carl Ewings! Cagey Carl! Cagey Carl!"

The doors are kicked open and my opponent comes trotting through, and the crowd goes absolutely berserk. Five times louder than when I walked in, that's for sure.

Cagey Carl.

"He looks about thirty years old!" I scream at Rube. He barely hears me.

"Yeah," he replies, "but he's a bit of a runt of a thing."

Nonetheless, however, he's still taller, stronger, and

faster-looking than me. He looks like he's been in a hundred fights and had fifty broken noses. Mostly though, he looks hard.

"Nineteen years old!" the old man continues into the mike. "Twenty-eight fights, twenty-four wins," and the big one — "twenty-two by knockout."

"Christ."

It's Rube who speaks this time, and Cagey Carl Ewings has jumped the ropes and circles the ring now like he wants to kill someone. And guess who just happens to be the closest guy around. It's me, of course, thinking, *Twenty-two knockouts. Twenty-two knockouts.* I'm dog's meat. I'm dog's meat, I swear it.

He comes over.

"Hey boy," he says.

"Hey," I answer, although I'm not sure he wants one. I'm just being friendly, really. You can't blame one for trying.

Whatever it is, it seems to work, because he smiles.

Then he states something very clearly.

He states, "I'm gonna kill you."

"Okay."

Did I just say that?

"You're scared." Another statement.

"If you like."

"Oh, I like, mate, but I'll like it even more when they cart you out of here on a stretcher."

"Is that right?"

"Definitely."

In the end, he smiles again and returns to his corner. Frankly, I'm quite sure he'll beat the skin off me. Cagey Carl. What an idiot, and I'd tell him so if I wasn't so afraid of him. Now there's only me and the fear and the furled footsteps I take to center ring. Rube stands behind me.

Now I feel naked, in just my dark blue shorts, my gymmies, and with the gloves on my hands. I feel too skinny, too bare. Like you can read the fear on me. The warm room filters across my back. The cigarette smoke breathes onto my skin. It smells like cancer.

Light is on us.

Blinding.

The crowd is dark.

Hidden.

They're just voices now. No names, no blondes, no beers or anything else. Just voices drawn toward the light, and there's no way to liken them to anything else. They sound like people gathered around a fight. That's all. That's what they are and they like what they are.

Both Carl and I sweat. There's Vaseline above his stare, which grinds its way into my eyes. It dawns on me very quickly that he really *does* want to kill me.

"Fair fight," the referee says, and that's all he says.

Then it's back to the corner.

My legs rage with anticipation.

My heart turns.

My head nods, as Rube gives me two instructions.

The first: "Don't go down."

The second: "If you do go down, be sure to get up."

"Okay."

Okay.

Okay.

What a word, ay? What a word, because you can't always mean it when you say it. Everything's gonna be okay. Yeah, whatever, because it's not. Everything hinges on you yourself, which in this case, is me.

"Okay," I say again, feeling the irony of it, and the bell rings and this is it.

Is it? I ask myself. *Is this it? Really?*

The answer to my question comes not from me, but from Cagey Carl, who has made his intentions excessively clear. He sprints over to me and throws out his left hand. I duck it, swing around, and get out of the corner.

He laughs as he chases me.

All round.

He comes at me, I duck.

He swings and misses and tells me I'm scared.

Toward the end of the round, his left glove finds its way through, echoing onto my jaw. Then his right finds me, and another one. Then the bell.

The round is over and I haven't thrown a single punch.

Rube tells me.

He says, "Just a hint you can't win a fight without throwing any punches."

"I know."

"Well?"

"Well what?"

"Well, start throwin' a few."

"All right." But personally, I'm just glad I survived the first round without being knocked down. I'm ecstatic that I'm still upright.

Second round. Still no punches, but this time, late, I hit the canvas and the crowd roars. Cagey Carl stands over me and says, "Hey boy! Hey boy!" That's all he says as I struggle to my knees and stand. Soon after, the bell rings. Everyone knows I'm scared.

This time Rube abuses me.

"If y' gonna carry on like this there's no point bein' here! Remember what we said that morning? This is our chance. Our *only* chance, and you're gonna blow it because you're scared of a little pain!" His face snarls at me. He barks. "If I was fightin' this guy I'd have dropped 'im in the first round and we both know it. It takes me twenty minutes to beat *you*, so get interested an' pull y' finger out, or go home!"

Yet still, I throw no punches.

Boos emerge from the crowd. No one likes a coward.

Rounds three and four, no punches.

Finally, the last round, the fifth.

What happens?

I walk out, my hammering heart smashing through

my ribs. I duck and swerve and Cagey Carl lands a few more good punches. He keeps telling me to stop running, but I don't. I keep running, and I survive my first fight. I lose it, on account of throwing no punches, and the crowd wants to lynch me. On my way out of the ring, they yell in my face, spit at me, and one guy even gives me a nice crack in the ribs. I deserve it.

Back in the room, the other fellas only shake their heads.

Perry ignores me.

Rube can't bring himself to look at me.

Instead, he punches the raw meat that hangs down around us as I take my gloves off, ashamed. There's another fight before Rube goes on. He punches hard and waits and we know. Rube will win. He has that about him now. I don't know where it came from — maybe that fight in the school yard. I'm not sure, but I can smell it, right up to the time when the other fight's over.

When Perry tells him, "It's time," Rube punches one last pig and we go to the doors. Again, we wait, and when Perry's voice comes to us, Rube bursts through the door.

Perry yells again: "And now, I think you'll see something tonight that you'll talk about for the rest of your life! You'll say that you saw him." All quiet. All quiet and Perry's voice lowers. Serious. "You'll say, 'I was there. I was there that first night when Ruben Wolfe fought. I saw Fighting Ruben Wolfe's first fight.' That's what you'll say. . . ."

Fighting Ruben Wolfe.

So that's his name.

Fighting Ruben Wolfe, and what the crowd does see is Rube walking toward the ring, in Steve's jacket. Like everyone else so far, they can smell it. The confidence. They see it in the eyes that peer out from his hood.

His walk is not bouncy or cocky.

He throws no punches to the air.

No step, however, is out of turn.

He is straight ahead, straight out, straight and hard, and ready to fight.

"Hope you're better than your brother," someone calls.

It hurts me. Wounds me.

"I am."

But not as much as that. Not as much as those two words from my own brother's lips, as he walks on, without flinching.

102

"I'm ready tonight," he talks on, and I am aware that now, he speaks only to himself. The crowd, Perry, me — we're all just out there somewhere, unfocused. Now it's just Rube, the fight, and the win. There is no world around it.

Typically, his opponent jumps into the ring, but that's about it. In the first round, Rube knocks him down twice. The bell saves him. In the break, all I do is give my brother some water as he sits and stares and waits. He waits for the fight with a slight smile, like there's nowhere else he'd rather be. He makes his legs rise and fall very slightly and very fast. He does it over, over, over again, before jumping up and going out, fists raised. Fighting.

The second round's the last round.

Rube catches him with a great right hand.

He punches his lungs out.

Then he goes under his ribs.

Even in the neck.

Shoulder.

Arm.

Anywhere legal and uncovered.

Finally, he goes straight through his face. Three times,

until the blood rants and raves on its way out of the
other guy's mouth.

"Stop it," Rube says to the ref.

The crowd roars.

"Stop the fight." But the ref has no intention to do so,
and Rube is forced to bury one last punch onto the
chin of Wizard Walter Brighton, and he falls cold to the
canvas.

All is loud and violent.

Beer glasses smash.

People shout.

A drop of extra blood hits the canvas.

Rubes stares.

Then another roar does a lap around the factory floor.

"That's it then," Rube says when he returns to the corner. "I told 'em to stop it but I guess they like the blood.
That's what people're payin' for, I s'pose."

He climbs out of the ring and is given instant worship
by the crowd. They pour beer on him, shake hands
with his glove, and yell out how great he is. Rube reacts
to none of them.

At the end of the night, we all file back into Perry's

van. Bumper won in five but the other blokes all lost, including me, of course. The ride home is all silent. Only two fighters hold a fifty-dollar note in their hand. The others have a little bit of tip money in their pockets, thrown into their corner at the end of the fight. All of them except me, that is. Like I've said, it's clear that no one likes a coward.

Perry drops everyone else off first and lets Rube and me out at Central.

"Hey Rube," he calls.

"Yeah."

"You can fight, boy. See y' next week."

"Same time?"

"Yeah."

Perry, to me: "Cameron, if you do what you did tonight next week, I'll kill you."

Me: "All right."

My heart falls to my ankles, the van takes off, and Rube and I walk home. I kick my heart along the ground. I feel like crying, but I don't. I wish I was Rube. I wish I was Fighting Ruben Wolfe and not the Underdog. I wish I was my brother.

A train passes above us as we walk through the tunnel and onto Elizabeth Street. The sound is deafening, then gone.

Our feet take over.

Out on the other side, on the street, I can smell the fear again. I can pick up the scent. It's easy to find, and Rube smells it too, I can sense it. But he doesn't know it. He doesn't feel it.

The worst part is the knowing that things have changed. See, Rube and I had always been together. We were both down low. We were both scrap. Both no good.

Now Rube's a winner, and I'm a Wolfe on my own. I'm the Underdog, alone.

On our way through the front gate back home, Rube pats me on the shoulder, twice. His previous anger has calmed, probably on account of his own great victory. We brace ourselves for the questions of why we're so late for dinner. It doesn't happen, as Mum's doing an evening shift at the hospital, and Dad's out walking. The first thing Rube does is hose the blood off his gloves in the backyard.

When he comes into our room, he says, "We'll have dinner and then walk Miffy, right?"

"Yeah."

My own gloves go straight back under my bed. They're spotless. Squeaky clean.

"Rube?"

"Yeah?"

"You've gotta tell me how it felt. Y' gotta tell me how it felt to win."

Quiet.

All quiet.

Voices of Mum and Dad wander down at us from the kitchen. They're talking to Steve, because I hear my brother's voice as well. Sarah sleeps in her own room, I guess.

"How'd it feel?" Rube asks himself. "I don't know exactly, but it made me wanna howl."

CHAPTER 9

"**G**rab that bag there," Steve tells me. Just like he said he would, he's moving out. All his stuff is cleared from the basement as he prepares to leave home, get a flat with his girl. He will rent for a while, I'd say, and then he'll probably buy something. He's been working a long while now. Good job, just started part-time university. Nice suits. Not bad for a few years out of school. He just says it's time to leave, with Mum and Dad struggling to pay bills, and Dad refusing the dole.

He isn't dramatic.

He doesn't look down into his room with a last nostalgic gaze.

He just smiles, gives Mum a hug, shakes Dad's hand, and walks out.

On the porch, Mum cries. Dad holds up his hand in good-bye. Sarah holds the last remnants of a hug in her arms. A son and brother is gone. Rube and I travel with him, to help him unpack what's left of his stuff. The flat he will live in is only about a kilometer away, but he says he wants to move south.

"Down near the National Park."

"Good idea."

"Fresh air and beaches."

"Sounds good."

We drive off and it's only me who turns around to see the rest of the Wolfe pack on the front porch. They will watch the car till it disappears. Then, one by one, they will go back inside. Behind the flyscreen. Behind the wooden door. Behind the walls. Into the world within the world.

"Bye Steve," we say, when all is unpacked.

"I'm only up the street for now," he says, and I reach for a semblance of recognition in his voice. Anything that sounds like *It's okay, lads. We'll be right. We all will be*. Steve's voice sounds nothing like it though. We all know that Steve will be okay. There's no irony in the word for him. Steven will always be okay. That's just how things are.

None of us embrace.

Steve and Rube shake hands.

Steve and I shake hands.

His last words are, "Make sure Mum's okay, right?"

"Right."

We run home, together, in the nearly-dark of Tuesday evening. Rube is waiting for me as we run. He pushes me. The next fight loiters around, like a thief, waiting to thieve. It's five days away.

Each night, I dream about it.

I nightmare.

I sweat.

In my dreams, I fight Perry. I fight Steve and Rube. Even my mother steps up and beats the hell out of me. The weirdest thing is that every time, my father is in the crowd, just watching. He says nothing. Does nothing. He simply watches everything go by, or reads the classifieds, looking for that elusive job.

On Saturday night, I hardly sleep at all.

All through Sunday, I mope around. I barely eat.

Like last week, Perry picks us up, but he takes us to Glebe this time, way down the end.

All is the same.

Same type of crowd.

Same guys, same blondes, same smell.

Same fear.

The warehouse is old and creaky, and the room we sit in is nearly falling apart.

Before the doors kick open, Rube reminds me.

"Remember. Either the other guy kills you, or Perry does. If I was you, I know who I'd prefer it to be."

I nod.

The doors.

They're open.

Perry shouts again and after a last deep breath, I enter the crowd. My opponent awaits me, but tonight, I don't even look at him. Not at the start. Not at the pre-match talk by the referee. Not ever.

The first time I see him is when he's in my face.

He's taller.

He has a small goatee.

He throws punches that are slow but hard.

I duck and swerve and get out of the way.

No suspense now.

No wondering.

I take one on my shoulder and counterpunch him. I get inside and throw a jab into his face. It misses. I throw another. It misses.

His giant hand seems to shake me first, then land on my chin. I hit him back, in the ribs.

"That's the way, Cam!" I hear Rube call out, and when the round is over, he smiles at me. "Even round," he tells me. "You can drop this clown easy." He even begins to laugh. "Just imagine you're fighting me."

"Good idea."

"You afraid of me?"

"A bit."

"Well, beat him anyway."

He gives me a last drink and I go out for the second. This time it's the crowd that swerves. Their voices climb through the ropes and wrap around me. When I'm on the canvas, they fall over me like a stream, making me get up.

The third is a nonevent. We both get tangled up and throw punches into the ribs. I hurt him once but he laughs at me.

In the fourth, he tells me something at the start. He says, "Hey, I had y' mother last night. She's pretty lousy,

112

ay. Pretty dirty." That's when I decide that I have to win. There's a picture in my mind of Mum, Mrs. Wolfe, working. Tired to the bone, but still working. For us. I don't lose my mind or go crazy, but I get more intense. I'm more patient, and when I get my chance, I land three good punches in his face. When the bell rings for the end of the round, I don't stop punching him.

"What the hell happened to you?" Rube laughs in our corner.

I answer, "Got hungry."

"Good."

In the fifth, I go down twice and the guy they call Thunder Joe Ross goes down once. Each time I hit the canvas, the crowd urges me to my feet, and when the bell rings and the decision is announced, they clap, and coins are thrown into my corner. Perry collects them.

I've lost the fight, but I have fought well.

I've risen to my feet.

That's all I had to do.

"There." Perry gives me every cent when we reach the dressing room. "Twenty-two bucks eighty. That's a good tip. Most losers are happy with fifteen or twenty."

"He ain't a loser."

The voice belongs to Rube, who is standing behind me.

"Whatever you say," Perry agrees (not caring if it's true or not), and he's gone.

When it comes to Rube's fight, the crowd is extra sharp. Their eyes are glued to him, watching his every move, every mannerism, every everything that might indicate what they've heard about him. Word has traveled fast that Perry Cole's got a hot new fighter, and everyone wants to see him. They don't see much.

His fight begins with a massive left hook.

The guy hits the ropes and Rube keeps going. He rinses the guy out. Whales him. His hands launch into his ribs. Uppercuts, one after the other. Midway through the round, it's all over.

"Get up!" people shout, but this guy just can't. He can barely move.

Rube stands there.

Above him.

He doesn't smile.

The crowd sees the blood, and they smell it. They look into Rube's fire-stomped eyes. Fighting Ruben

Wolfe. It's a name they will come to see here now for a long time.

Again, when he climbs out of the ring, they smother him.

Drunk men.

Horny women.

They all rub up against him. They all try to touch him, and Rube remains as he is. He walks straight through them, smiling out of obligation and thanking them, but never losing the concentration on his face.

Sitting in the room, he says to me, "We did good today, Cam."

"Yeah, we did."

Perry gives him his fifty. "No tip for the winner," he says. "He gets his fifty anyway."

"No worries."

When Rube stands and goes to the toilet, Perry and I have words together.

"They love him," he explains. "Just like I thought." A pause. "You know why?"

"Yep." I nod.

He tells me anyway. "It's because he's tall and he's got

looks and he can fight. And he's hungry. That's what they like most." He grins. "The women out there are begging me to tell 'em where I found him. They love fellas like Rube."

"It's to be expected."

Outside, when we leave, there's a blonde thing hanging round.

"Hey Ruben." She tiptoes over. "I like the way you fight."

We walk on and she follows and her arm touches slightly with his. Meanwhile, I look at her. All of her.

Eyes, legs, hair, neck, breath, eyebrows, breasts, ankles, front zipper, shirt, buttons, earrings, arms, fingers, hands, heart, mouth, teeth, and lips.

She's great.

Great, dumb, and stupid.

Next, I'm shocked.

Shocked, because my brother stops and they look at each other. Next thing she has him in her mouth. She's swallowing his lips. They're against the wall. Girl, Rube, wall. Pushed up against each other. Merging. He kisses her hard for a fair while. Open tongue, hands everywhere.

Then he stops and walks away.

Rube walks on and says, "Thanks, love."

"Hey Rube. Y' awake again?"

"As usual. Do you ever shut up of a night?"

"Not lately."

"Well, I guess you've got an excuse this time — you fought real well."

"Where's the next one on at?"

"Ashfield, I think, then Helensburgh."

"Rube?"

"What now?"

"Why haven't y' moved into Steve's room?"

"Why haven't you?"

"Why hasn't Sarah?"

"I think Mum wants to turn it into like an office, for doin' paperwork and that kind of thing. That's what she said, anyway."

I say, "And it wouldn't feel right, I don't reckon."

The basement is Steve's room and it always will be. He's moved on but the rest of the Wolfe family stay as they are. They need to. I feel it in the dusty night air, and I taste it.

I also have another question.

I don't ask it.

I can't bring myself.

It's that girl.

I think about it but I don't ask it.

There are some things you just don't ask.

CHAPTER 10

We train and fight and keep training, and I get my first win up. It's down in Helensburgh, against some low-life yobbo who keeps calling me cowboy.

"That all y' got, cowboy, huh?"

"You hit like my mother, cowboy."

All that kind of thing.

I put him down once in the third and twice in the fifth. I win it on points. Fifty dollars, but more importantly, a win. A sniff of victory for the Underdog. It feels great, especially at the end, when Rube smiles at me and I smile back.

"I'm proud a' you."

That's what he says afterward, in the dressing room, before concentrating again.

Later, he worries me.

He . . . I don't know.

I notice a deliberate change in my brother. He's harder. He has a switch, and once a fight comes near, he flicks it and he is no longer my brother Rube. He's a machine. He's a Steve, but different. More violent. Steve's a winner because he's always been a winner. Rube's a winner because he wants to beat the loser out of himself. Steve *knows* he's a winner, but I think Rube's still trying to prove it to himself. He's fiercer, more fiery, ready to beat all loss from his vision.

He's Fighting Ruben Wolfe.

Or is he actually *fighting* Ruben Wolfe?

Inside him.

Proving himself.

To himself.

I don't know.

It's in each eye.

The question.

Each breath.

Who's fighting who?

Each hope.

In the ring tonight, he leaves his opponent in pieces. The other guy is barely there, from the very beginning.

Rube has something over all of them. His desire is severe, and his fists are fast. Every time the guy goes down, Rube stands over him tonight, and he tells him.

"Get up."

Again.

"Get up."

By the third one, he can't.

This time, Rube screams at him.

"Get up, boy!"

He lays into the padding in the corner and kicks it before climbing back out.

In the dressing room Rube doesn't look at me. He speaks words that are not directed at anyone. He says, "Another one, ay. Two rounds and he's on the deck."

More women like him.

I see them watching him.

They're young and trashy and good-looking. They like tough fellas, even though guys like that are likely to treat them poorly. I guess women are only human too. They're as stupid as us sometimes. They seem to like the bad ones a bit.

But is Rube bad? I ask myself.

It's a good question.

He's my brother.

Maybe that's all I know.

As weeks edge past us, he fights and wins and he doesn't bother shaving. He turns up and wins. Turns up and wins. He only smiles when *I* fight well.

At school, there's a new air about him. People know him. They recognize him. They know he's tough, and people have heard. They know he does fight nights, though none of them know that I do. It's for the best, I s'pose. If they saw me fight, it would only make them laugh. I would be Rube's sidekick. They'd say, *Go watch them Wolfes fight, ay. The younger one, what's his name, he's a joke, but Ruben can fight like there's no to-morrow.*

"It's all rumors," is what Rube tells people. "I don't fight anywhere except in my backyard." He lies well. "Look at the bruises on my brother. We fight all the time at home, but that's it. No more than that."

One Saturday morning, a colder one than normal, but clear, we go out for a run. The sun's barely coming up, and as we run, we see some fellas just coming home. They've been out all night.

"Hey Rubey!" one yells.

It's an old mate of Rube's named Cheese. (Well, at least, his nickname's Cheese, anyway. I don't think anyone knows his real name.) He's standing on the walkway up to Central Station with a giant pumpkin under his arm.

"Hey Cheeser." Rube raises his head. We walk up toward him. "What y' been doin' lately?"

"Ah, nothin' much. Just livin' in a drunken haze, ay. Since I left school, all I do is work and drink."

"Yeah?"

"It's good, mate."

"Enjoyin' it?"

"Lovin' every minute."

"That's what I like to hear." But really, my brother doesn't care. He scratches his two-day growth. "So what's the go with the pumpkin?"

"Been hearin' you're a bit of a gunfighter these days."

"Nah, just in the backyard." Rube recalls something. "You of all people should know that."

"Yeah mate, certainly," because Cheese used to be in our yard sometimes when we got the gloves out. He remembers the pumpkin he's holding. He lifts it back into the conversation. "Found this in an alley, so we're gonna play football with it." His mates arrive, around the three of us.

"About here, Cheese?" they ask.

"Why, certainly," and he gives the pumpkin a good kick down the walkway. Someone chases it then and comes running back with it.

"Belt him!" someone else yells, and it's on. Teams divide quickly, the fella gets belted, and pieces of pumpkin go flying all over the place.

"Rube!" I call for it.

He passes.

I drop it.

"Ah, y' useless bloody turkey!" Cheese laughs. Do people still use that word? It's a word people's grandfathers use. In any case, I erase my disappointment by tackling the next guy into the concrete.

A bag lady walks past, checking things out for breakfast.

Then a few couples get out of the way.

The pumpkin's in half. We continue with one of them, and the other half is squashed against the wall under the money machine.

Rube gets belted.

I get belted.

Everyone does, and all around us, there's the stench of sweat, raw pumpkin, and beer.

"You blokes stink," Rube tells Cheese.

"Why thank you," Cheese responds.

We keep going, until the pumpkin's the size of a golf ball. That's when the cops show up.

They walk up, a man and a woman, smiling.

"Boys," the bloke cop opens with. "How's it going?"

"Tosser Gary!" Rube calls out. "What are *you* doin' here?"

Yes, you've guessed right. The cops are our mates from the dog track. Gary, the corrupt, bet-placing male cop, and Cassy, the brilliant brunette gorgeous cop.

"Ahh, *you!*" the cop laughs. "Been down the track lately?"

"Nah," Rube answers. "Been a bit busy."

Cassy nudges Gary.

He pauses.

Remembers.

His job.

"Now fellas," he begins, and we all know what he'll

say. "You know this kind of thing isn't on. There's pumpkin all over the place and when the sun hits it, it's gonna stink like my old man's work boots."

Silence.

Then a few yeahs.

Yeah this, yeah that, and a yeah you're right I s'pose.

But no one understands, not really.

No one cares.

I'm wrong.

I'm wrong because I find myself stepping forward, saying, "Okay Gary, I know what y' mean," and start picking up pieces of pumpkin. Silently, Rube follows. The others, drunk, only watch. Cheese helps a bit, but none of the others do anything. They're too shocked. Too drunk. Too out of breath. Too stoned.

"Thanks a lot," Gary and Cassy say when we're done and our drunken friends are on their way.

"I think I'd love to beat the hell out of some of those fellas," Rube mentions. His words are offhand, but fierce. Like he'd do it if the cops would turn their backs for a minute.

Gary looks at him.

A few times.

He notices.

He says it.

"You've changed mate. What's happened?"

All Rube says is, "I don't know."

Neither do I.

It's a conversation with myself at Central Station. It goes on inside my head as Rube and Gary talk a little further.

It goes like this:

"Hey Cameron?"

"What?"

"Why does he scare you all of a sudden?"

"He's fierce now, and even when he smiles and laughs, he stops it real fast and concentrates again."

"Maybe he just wants to be somebody."

"Maybe he wants to kill somebody."

"Now you're bein' stupid."

"All right."

"Maybe he's just sick of losin' and never wants to feel it again."

"Or maybe he's the one that's afraid."

"Maybe."

"But afraid of what?"

"I don't know. What can a winner be afraid of?"

"Losing?"

"No, it's more than just that. I can tell...."

"All the same, though, Cassy looks great, doesn't she?"

"She sure does...."

"But afraid of what?"

"I told you. I don't know."

CHAPTER 11

I only know that I'm a new kind of afraid.

You know how dogs whine when they're afraid, like when a storm's coming? Well, I feel like doing it right now. I feel like asking questions, in desperation.

When did this happen?

How did it happen?

Why did he change so quickly?

Why aren't I happy for him?

Why does it scare me?

And why can't I put my finger on exactly what it is?

All of those questions swing through me, eroding me a little each time. They swing through me during my brother's next few fights. All knockouts. They swing through me each time he stands over his man, telling him to get up, and when the people touch him to grab a little piece of his greatness. I ask the same questions in the dressing room, among the smell of liniment and gloves and sweat. I ask them the next time I see Rube get it off with a nineteen-year-old uni student behind the Maroubra factory, before he walks away from her (without looking back). Then the next time a different girl. Then the next. I ask the questions at home when we eat our dinner with Mum pouring out the soup, and Sarah eating it politely, and Dad eating more failure with his meal. Putting it in his mouth. Chewing it. Tasting it. Swallowing it. Digesting it. Getting used to it. I ask them when Sarah and I wrestle some washing off the line. ("Damn it!" she yells. "It's raining! Hey Cam! Come help us get the washing off!" Just lovely, the two of us sprinting out back and ripping it all off the line, not caring if it's in shreds, just as long as it's bloody dry.) I even ask the questions when I smell my socks to see if they can go one more day or if I should wash them next shower. I ask them when I go and visit Steve at his new place and he gives me a cup of black coffee and a silent, friendly conversation.

Finally, someone else arrives to help me out a bit.

It's Mrs. Wolfe, who, thankfully, has some questions of her own. The best thing about this is that maybe she can get something out of Rube to help me understand him better. Also, she has chosen a night and a week in which I've won my last fight, so I don't have any bruises on me.

It's a Wednesday night, and Rube and I sit on our front porch with Miffy, patting him after his walk. The little wonder dog laps up the attention on the old lounge. He rolls on his stomach as Rube and I pat him and laugh at his ridiculous little fangs and claws.

"Oh Miffy!" Rube breathes out, and it's the shadow of his former callings for the dog when we used to pick him up. He only laughs now with something inside the voice of his throat.

What is it?

Regret?

Remorse?

Anger?

I don't know, but Mrs. Wolfe, she can sense it as well, and she has joined us now on the front porch, in the cold, dim light.

I love Mrs. Wolfe.

I've gotta tell you that right now.

I love Mrs. Wolfe because she's brilliant and she's a

genius even though her cooking's downright oppressive. I love her because she fights like hell. She fights better than Rube. Even Rube will tell you that — though her fight has nothing to do with fists. But it has plenty to do with blood. . . .

Her words tonight are these:

"What's up boys? Why are you always coming home so late on Sundays?" She smiles, alone. "I know that you were going down to the dog track not so long ago. You're aware of that, aren't you?"

I look at her. "How'd y' find that out?"

"Mrs. Craddock," she confesses.

"Bloody Craddock!" I yelp. Mrs. Craddock, a neighbor of ours, was always at the dogs, chewing a hot dog with her false teeth, and sinking Carlton Cold beer like there was no tomorrow. Not to mention smoking Long Beach 25s till the cows came home.

"Forget the dogs," Mum sighs.

She talks.

We listen.

We have to.

When you love and respect someone, you listen.

"Now, I know things are rough at the moment, fellas,

but just do me a favor and come home at a decent hour. Try to get here before dark."

I break.

"Okay Mum."

Rube doesn't.

He says, straight and hard, "We've been goin' down to the gym. Sunday afternoons it's cheaper, and you can learn boxing."

Boxing.

Nice one, Rube.

We know how Mum feels about boxing.

"Is that what you want to do?" she asks, and her mild tone is surprising. I think she knows she can't stop us. She knows the only way is to let us find out. She continues and ends with two words. "Boxing? Really?"

"It's safe. All supervised and taken care of. Not like we used to do in the backyard. None of the one-handed rubbish."

Which isn't a lie. Yes, the fights *are* supervised and taken care of, but by whom? It's funny how truth and lies can come in the same clothes. They wear flanno shirts, gym boots, jeans, and Ruben Wolfe's lips.

"Just look after each other."

"We will," and I smile at Mrs. Wolfe because I want her to think that everything's all right. I want her going to work without worrying about us. She deserves at least that.

Rube gives her an "Okay."

"Good."

"We'll try to get back quicker," he goes on, before Mum returns inside. First she pats Miffy for a while, running her dry fingers through our friend's soft, fluffy fur.

"Look at this dog," I say once she's gone. Just to say something. Anything.

"What about him?"

I'm lost, and unsure what to say. "I guess, we've got to liking him, ay."

"But what does liking do?" Rube looks at the road. "It doesn't do anything."

"Does hating?"

"What have we got to hate?" He's laughing now.

The truth is, there's a lot to hate, and a lot to love.

Love.

The people.

Hate.

The situation.

Behind us we hear Mum cleaning up the kitchen. We turn and see the silhouette of our dad helping her. We see him kiss her on the cheek.

He is unemployed.

He still loves her.

She loves him.

Watching it, I see the handful of fights that Rube and I have had inside the warehouses and factories. They're pale, I decide. Pale in comparison. There's a vision also of Sarah, putting overtime in (as she's been known to do lately), or even just watching TV or reading. There's even a vision of Steve, out there on his own, living. Mainly though, it's Mum and Dad. Mr. and Mrs. Wolfe.

I think about Fighting Ruben Wolfe.

I think about fighting Ruben Wolfe.

From the inside.

I think about finding Ruben Wolfe. . . .

I think about fights you know you'll win, fights you know you'll lose, and the fights you just don't know about. I think about the ones in between.

It's me now who looks at the road.

I speak.

Talk.

Say it.

I say, "Don't lose your heart, Rube."

And very clearly, without moving, my brother answers me.

He says, "I'm not tryin' to lose it, Cam. I'm tryin' to find it."

Tonight, there's nothing.

There's no "Hey Rube, are you awake?"

No "Of course I bloody am!"

There's just silence.

Silence, Rube and me.

And the darkness.

He's awake, though. I can sense it. I can feel it, just out of reach from my vision.

There are no voices from the kitchen.

There's no world but this one.

This room.

This air.

This awake-ness.

CHAPTER 12

I n the half-consciousness of Saturday morning, I'm
dreaming of women, flesh, and fights.

The first fills me with fear.

The second fills me with thrill.

The third fills me with more fear.

My blanket covers me. Only my human snout sticks
out the top, allowing me to breathe.

"We goin' for a run?" I ask across to Rube.

Is he still asleep?

"Rube?"

An answer. "Nah, not today."

Good, I think. *This blanket might be full of fear, but
it's still pretty warm under here. Besides, I reckon we
could use a rest.*

"I wanna do a bit of work later though," Rube continues. "Gotta work on my jab. Can we do some One Punch later in the backyard?"

"I thought we were finished with that. Like you said to Mum."

"Well, we're not. I've changed my mind." He rolls over but still talks. "You could use some work on your own jab too, y' know." He's right.

"Okay."

"So stop whingein'."

"I don't mind." It's the truth. "It'll be fun anyway. Like the old days."

"Damn right."

"Good."

We return to sleep. For me, it's back to the flesh, fighting, and women. *What's it back to for Rube?* I wonder.

Once we're up and the day progresses, Mum, Dad, and Sarah go to Steve's place, to see how he's going. It's our golden opportunity to train. We take it.

As we always do now, we go over and get Miffy.

From our back step, the pooch looks up at us. He licks his lips.

We circle the yard.

Rube hits me, but I hit back. He gets more in than me, but about every second punch Rube gets in, I get one back. He becomes a little frustrated.

When we have a break, he says, "I've gotta be quicker. Quicker once the jab goes out. Quicker to block."

"Yeah, but what happens in your fights," I tell him, "is that you throw a jab or two and follow it with your left. Your left's always quicker than the counterpunch."

"I know, but what if I come up against a real good counterpuncher? Then I'm in trouble."

"I doubt it."

"Do y'?"

From there, we practice more and then swap gloves for a bit of fun. Back to the old days all right. One glove each, circling the backyard, each throwing punches. Smiling at hitting. Smiling at being hit. We don't go all out, because we both have to fight tomorrow, so there are no bruises and no blood. *It's funny*, I think, as we crouch and I watch Rube, who also crouches with that look on his face. Just content. *It's funny when we fight one-handed in our backyard, that's when I feel closest to my brother. That's when it feels strongest that we're broth-*   .

ers and always will be. I feel it, watching him, and when he gives me a slight Ruben Wolfe grin, Miffy flings himself at him, and Rube mock-fights him, letting Miffy curl around his solitary glove.

"Bloody Miffy," he smirks. There are glimpses.

Later, the tempo changes back to what has become normal.

We're sitting in our room, and Rube pulls open the wretched corner of carpet next to my bed. In one envelope is his money. In the other is mine. Rube's envelope holds three hundred and fifty dollars. Mine holds about one sixty. Rube has won seven fights from seven starts. My own money comes from two wins and the rest of it is tips.

Rube sits on his bed and counts his money.

"All there?" I inquire.

"Why wouldn't it be?"

"I was only bloody askin'!"

He looks at me.

Thinking about it, it's actually the first time in a while that either of us has raised his voice in real anger at the other. We used to do it all the time. It was normal.

Almost fun. A regular occurrence. Today, however, it's like a bullet, buried deep into the flesh of our brotherhood. It's a bullet of doubt, a bullet of not knowing.

Outside the window, the city counts the seconds, as we sit there in silence.

One — two — three — four —

More words get to their feet.

They belong to Rube.

He says, "Are the dogs on today?"

"I think so, yeah. Saturday the eighth. Yep, that's today."

"You wanna go down?"

"Yeah, why not?" I smile. "We might see those cops again and have a laugh."

"Yeah, they're all right, those two."

I take a handful of my tip change and chuck some of it Rube's way.

"Thanks."

I put ten bucks in my jacket pocket. "No worries."

We put our shoes on and leave the house. We write a note saying we'll be back before dark, and place it on the kitchen table. It goes next to the *Herald*. That paper — it sits there, open at the employment section. It sits there like a war, and each small advertisement is another trench for a person to dive into. To hope and fight in.

We stare at it.

We pause.

We know.

Rube drinks some milk out of the carton, puts it back in the fridge, and we walk out, leaving the war on the table, with the note.

Outside, we walk.

Out on the front door and beyond the gate.

We're in our usual gear. We're jeaned, flanno-ed, gymmied, and jacketed. Rube's jacket is corduroy. It's brown and old and ridiculous, but typically, he looks downright brilliant in it. Mine's my black spray jacket, and I'd say I look about okay. Or at least, I hope. Somewhere on the border of it anyway.

We walk, and the smell of street is raucous. It shoots through me and I enjoy it. The city buildings in the distance are holding up the sky, it seems. The sky is blue and bright, and the strides of Rube and I walk toward it. We used to languish when we walked, or sidle down the street like dogs that have just done something wrong. Now Rube walks upright, because he's on the attack.

143

We get to the track and it's about one o'clock.

"Look," I point. "It's Mrs. Craddock."

As expected, she's sitting in the stand, holding a hot dog in one hand and balancing a coldie and a cigarette in the other. The smoke smothers her and divides either side.

"Hi fellas," she calls to us, moving the cigarette to her lips. Or is she taking a chug on the beer? She has brown-gray hair, purple lipstick, a scrunched nose, and wears an old dress and thongs. She's big. A big woman.

"Hey Mrs. Craddock," we greet her. (It was the beer she was after, *then* a quick inhalation.) "How y' goin'?"

"Beautifully, thanks. Nothin' better than a day with the dogs."

"That's for sure." But I'm thinking, *Whatever y' say, love.* "Who do y' like in the next one?"

She grins.

Oh man. It's not pretty. Those falsies . . .

"Number two," she advises. "Peach Sunday."

Peach Sunday. Peach Sunday? What sort of person calls a greyhound Peach Sunday? They should get together with whoever called that other dog You Bastard.

"Can she gallop?" I ask.

"That's horses, love," Craddock answers. See how in-furiating she is? Can she really think that *I* think I'm at the horse track? "And it's a he."

"Well?" Rube asks. "Is he a certainty?"

"Sure as I'm sittin' here."

"Well, she's sittin' here all right." Rube nudges me on our way. "All three hundred pounds of her."

We turn and bid her good-bye.

Me: "Bye, Mrs. Craddock."

Rube: "Yeah, see y' later. Thanks for the tip."

We look around. Our cop mates aren't here, so we have to hunt for someone else to put the bet on for us. It won't be hard. A voice finds us.

"Hey Wolves!"

It's Perry Cole, holding his customary beer, as well as a grin. "What are a couple of respectable young lads such as yourselves doin' down here?"

"Just puttin' a few on," Rube replies. "Can y' slap a bet on for us?"

"Of course."

"Race three, number two."

"Right."

He puts it on for us and we go down to the sunny part

of the grandstand, where Perry sits in a big group. He introduces us, tells everyone what gunfighters we are (or Rube, at least), and we watch. There are some ugly guys and girls there, but some nice girls too. One of them is our age and pretty. Dark hair, cut short. Eyes of sky. She's skinny and she smiles at us, polite and shy.

"That's Stephanie," Perry tells us as he rattles through the names. Her face is tanned and sweet. Her neck and throat are smooth, and she wears a pale blue shirt, a bracelet, and old jeans. She's got gymmies on, like us. I notice her arms and her wrists and her hands and fingers. They're feminine and beautiful and delicate. No rings. Just the bracelet.

All the other people talk, behind us.

So where do y' live? I ask, inside. No words come out.

"So, where do y' live?" Rube asks her, but his voice is so different from the voice that I would have used. His is said to be said. Not said to be nice.

"Glebe."

"Nice area."

Me, I say nothing.

I only look at her and her lips and her straight white teeth when she speaks. I watch the breeze run its fingers through her hair. I watch it breathe onto her neck. I even watch the air go into her mouth. Into her lungs, and back out . . .

She and Rube talk about regular things. School. Home. Friends. What bands they've seen lately of which Rube has seen none. He just makes it up.

Me?

I would never lie to her.

I promise.

"Go!"

It's everyone yelling as the dogs get let out and take off around the track.

"Go Peach Sunday!"

Rube stands and yells with the rest of the people.

"Go Peaches! Go son!"

As he does so, I look at Stephanie. Peach Sunday doesn't concern me anymore, even when he wins by two lengths and Rube slaps me on the back, and Perry slaps us *both* on the back.

"Old Craddock's all right then, ay!" Rube shouts at me, and faintly, I smile. Stephanie smiles also, at both of us. We've just made sixty-five dollars. Our first real win at the track. Perry collects it for us.

We decide to stay ahead from there and we just hang around and watch for the rest of the afternoon, till the shadows grow long and lean. When the crowd disperses after the last race, Perry invites us to his place for what he calls, "Food, drinks, and anything else you might need."

"No thanks." It's Rube. "We've gotta get home."

At that moment, Steph talks to an older girl I assume is her sister. They talk, then separate, and Steph is on her own.

Walking out the gate, I see her and say to Rube, "Shouldn't we walk with her or somethin'? You know, to make sure she doesn't get clocked on the way home. There are some good weirdos around here."

"We gotta be home before dark."

"Yeah, but —"

"Well, go if y' want," he urges me. "I'll tell Mum you'll be in a bit later. You just stopped by a mate's place."

I stop.

"Come on," he says, "make up y' mind."

I pause, go one way, then the other. I decide.

I run across the road, and once I turn to see where

Rube is, he's gone. I can't find him anywhere. Steph's walking up ahead. I catch up.

"Hey." Words. *More words*, I tell myself. *Gotta say more words.* "Hey Steph, can I walk with you?" *To make sure you get home all right*, I think, but I don't say it. It's just not something I would say. I can only hope she knows what I mean.

"Okay," she replies. "But isn't this out of your way?"

"Ah, not really."

It grows darker and there are no more words. It's just, I have no idea what to say, or what to talk about. The only thing that makes a sound is my heartbeat, stumbling through my body as we keep going. Our walk is slow. I look at her. She looks at me a few times too. Damn, she's beautiful. I see it under the streetlights — a world of sky in each eye, and the dark, short waves of hair and tanned skin.

It's cold.

God, she must be cold, and I take my jacket off and offer it to her. Still no words. Just my face, begging her to accept it. She does and she says, "Thanks."

At her gate, she asks, "You wanna come in? You can have something to drink."

"Oh nah," I explain. Quiet. Too quiet! "I have to get home. I wish I could though."

She smiles.

She smiles and takes the jacket off. When she hands it to me, I wish I could touch her fingers. I wish I could kiss her hand. I wish I could feel her lips.

"Thanks," she says again, and when she turns and walks toward her front door, I only stand and look at her. I take all of her in. Her hair, neck, shoulders. Her back. Her jeans and her legs, walking. Her hands again, the bracelet and her fingers. Then her last smile, when she says, "Hey Cameron."

"Yeah?"

"I might see y' tomorrow. I think I'll come down and have a look in the warehouse, even though I hate fights." She pauses a moment. "I hate betting at the dog track as well. I only go because the dogs are beautiful."

I stand there.

Still.

I wonder, *Can a Wolfe be beautiful?* However, "That's nice," is what I say. We connect. Her eyes pull mine into hers.

"So yeah," she says. "I'll try to make it there."

"Okay."

Then, "Hey, just out of interest," she asks. She considers something. "Is Rube as good a fighter as everyone says?"

I nod.

Just honestly.

"Yeah," I say. "He is."

"How 'bout you?"

"Me? I'm not much really. . . ."

There's one more smile and she says, "Might see you tomorrow then."

"All right," I reply. "I hope so."

There's a final turn and she's gone inside.

Once I'm alone, I stand a few more seconds and take off for home. I start running, from the adrenaline juice I taste in my throat.

Can a Wolfe be beautiful?

Can a Wolfe be beautiful?

I ask it as I run, with her image gathered in my mind. *I think Rube can be,* I answer, *when he's in the ring. He's handsome, yet ferocious, yet devastating, yet beautiful and handsome all over again.*

At home, I make it in time for dinner.

She's there, at the table with me. Stephanie. Steph. Eyes of sky. Sweet wrists and fingers, and waves of dark hair, and her love for the beautiful dogs at the track.

She might be there tomorrow.

She might be there.

She might be.

She might.

She.

I'm kidding, aren't I?

Cameron Wolfe.

Cameron Wolfe, and another girl who has shown just the slightest interest. And he loves her already. He's already prepared to fall all over her and beg her and vow to treat her right and do anything she wants. He's ready to give all of himself.

He's one boy, and surely, it is pain that looms, not bliss.

Or will this be different?

Can it be?

Will it be?

I don't know.

I anticipate and hope. I think about it all night. Even in bed, she's under my blanket with me.

Across the room, Rube's counting his money again.

Holding it out before him, he stares at it, like he's convincing himself of something.

I stare now as well, curious about what he sees.

"See this money," he says. "It's not three hundred and fifty dollars." He stares harder. "It's seven wins."

"Hey Rube?"

Nothing.

"Hey Rube? Rube?"

Tonight it's just her and me, under my blanket.

Visions echo.

They're played out on the ceiling, as hope grows inside me.

There are gold snippets of future in the darkness of the dark.

One last try:

"Hey Rube? Rube?"

Nothing.

All I have is the hope that I will fight well tomorrow and that she'll be there.

But she hates fights, I tell myself. So why would she come? More questions. Would she really come just to see me?

The visions are everywhere.

The answers are nowhere.

Yet, in the dead of night, in the listening dark, Rube says a very strange thing. Something I won't really understand until later.

He says, "Y' know, Cam, I've thought about it, and I think I like your money better than mine."

And I'm left lying there, in bed, thinking but not speaking. Just thinking.

CHAPTER 13

Sometimes I wish I had better fists on me. *Faster ones*, with faster arms and stronger shoulders. Usually I'm in bed when I think of that kind of thing, although today, I'm in the dressing room waiting for the call. I don't know. I just wish to be formidable. I wish I could walk through the crowd and climb into the ring to win, not just to fight.

"Cameron."

I wish I could look my opponent in the eye and tell him I'm going to kill him.

"Cameron."

I wish I could stand above him and tell him to get to his feet.

"Cameron!"

Finally, Rube has made it into my thoughts. He has hit me on the shoulder to burst through my mind. I still sit there, in my spray jacket, shivering. My gloves hang from my hands like dead weight, and I feel like falling to pieces.

"Are you fighting or what?" Rube shakes me.

She's out there, I think, and for once, I actually say it. To my brother. Quietly. "She's out there, Rube."

He looks at me closer, wondering who I'm talking about. "She is," I go on.

"Who?"

"That Steph, y' know the one?"

"*Who?*"

Oh, what's the point! I exclaim inside me.

Yet, I still speak softly. "Steph from the track."

"So what?" He's frustrated now, and close to picking me up and throwing me out into the crowd.

"So everything," I keep talking. I'm still vacant. Exhausted. "I saw her just a few minutes ago when I took a peek out the door."

Rube walks away. "Oh God almighty." He walks away and comes back. He's calm now. "Just get out there."

"Okay." But no movement.

Still calm. "Get out."

"All right," and I know that I must.

I stand up, the doors are kicked open, and I walk into the crowd. It's a crowd in which every person has the same face. It's her. Stephanie.

All is blur.

All confusion.

Perry, shouting.

The ref.

Keep it clean, fellas.

Fair fight.

Okay.

Do it.

Don't go down.

If you do go down, get up.

The bell, the fists, the fight.

It begins, and the first round is death.

The second round is the coffin.

The third is the funeral.

My opponent is not such a great fighter, but I'm not on today. I'm not up. I'm so scared of failing that I have accepted it. I've given in to it, almost as if I won't try because it will only make things worse.

"Get up!" screams Rube's distorted voice the first time I'm down. Somehow, I do it.

The second time, it's just the look in his eyes that makes me find my feet again. My legs ache and I stagger, over to the ropes. Hanging on. Hanging on.

The third time, I see her. I see her and it's only her. The rest of the crowd has disappeared and only Stephanie stands there, watching. The whole place is empty but for her. Her eyes are swimming with beauty and her stance makes me lunge for her, in an attempt for her to help me up.

"I only go because the dogs are beautiful," I hear her say.

What a strange thing to say, I think, then realize it's yesterday's voice that I hear. Today, she stands in silence, staring at me with solemn lips, closed up, as I struggle to my feet.

In the fourth round, I fight back. I rise up.

I navigate my head away from the other guy's fists and get in a few shots of my own. Blood has flooded my chest and stomach. It eats into my shorts.

Dog's blood.

A beautiful dog?

Who knows, because in the fifth round, I get knocked

out, and it isn't just one where I can't get up. It's a knockout where I'm knocked cold, unconscious.

When I'm out, she fills me.

I see her and we're at the track, just us in the grandstand, and she kisses me. She comes close and she tastes so nice. It's unbearable. Me, with one gentle hand on her face and the other nervously gripping the collar of her shirt. Her with her lips on mine, and her hands gliding up my rib cage, bit by bit. Just gentle, so gentle.

Her lips.

Her hips.

Her pulse, inside mine.

So gentle, so gentle.

So

"Gentle," I hear Rube's voice. "Be gentle with him."

Damn, I'm awake.

Awake and ashamed.

After a while, I'm on my feet again, but I'm slumped between Rube and Bumper, who has kindly jumped into the ring to help us out. "You right, little fella?" he asks.

"Yeah," I lie. "I'm right," and Rube and Bumper help me out of the ring.

It's darker in here now and my sight is paralyzed. Tonight it's shame that flows down my side, as the fluorescent lights hit me. They scratch my eyes out. They blind me.

Once out of the ring, I stop. I have to.

"What?" Rube questions me. "What's up? C'mon, we gotta get you back in the room."

"No," I say. "I've gotta walk on my own."

Rube's eyes search inside me then and something happens. His hands drop and he nods at me with such intensity that I nod ever so slightly back. Feeling grabs me, turns through me, and I walk.

We all do.

I walk with Rube and Bumper on either side of me, and the crowd is silent. The blood is drying onto my skin. My legs move forward. Once more. Once more. *Just keep walking*, I tell myself. *Head up. Head up*, I chant, *but still concentrate on y' feet. Don't fall down.*

There is no applause.

Just people, watching.

Just Stephanie, out there somewhere, watching.

Just Rube's proud eyes, as he walks next to me . . .

"The door," he says to Perry, and Perry opens it, when we get there. On the other side, I fall down again, swallowing my blood and turning over to grin at the ceiling. It drops and squashes me, then rises up and does it again.

"Rube," I call out, but he's miles away. "Rube . . ." A shout now. "Rube, are y' there?"

"I'm here brother."

Brother.

It makes me smile.

I say, "Thanks Rube. Thanks."

"It's all right brother."

Again with the *brother*.

Another smile on my lips.

"Did I win?" I ask, because now, I can't feel anything. I'm one with the floor.

"Nah mate." He won't lie. "You got hurt pretty bad, ay."

"Did I?"

"You did."

Slowly, I regain edges of composure. I clean myself up and watch Rube's fight through a gap in the door. Bumper's in his corner in my absence, even though my brother doesn't need him. I see Stephanie, swaying with the rest of the crowd, just watching when Rube knocks down his man in the second. I see her smile and it's a beautiful smile. But it's not a grandstand smile. It's not a smile for me. I have drowned in those eyes. I have vanished in the sky. And there I am, remembering that she doesn't really like fights. . . .

The bout ends later in the round.

The girl ends two minutes after it.

She ends when Rube goes past and she says something to him. Rube nods. It makes me wonder. *Has she asked if Cameron's okay? Does she want to see me?*

The thing is, though, that I can tell. Her eyes cannot be for me.

Or can they?

Soon we'll know, because during the next fight, Rube goes out the back door, and listening, I can tell he's talking to her. He's talking to Stephanie.

I'm close. Too close, but I can't help it. I have to listen. It starts with Rube's voice.

"You wanna see if my brother's okay, do you?"

Silence.

"Well, do y'?"

"Is he all right?"

I'm in her voice for a brief moment, letting it cover me, smother me, until Rube sees things clearly. He says it hard.

"Y' don't care, isn't that right?"

"Of course I do!"

"Y' *don't*." Rube's made up his mind. "Y' came for me, didn't you?" A gap. "*Did*n't you?"

"No, I —"

"See, there are smart girls out there somewhere, and they're not here. They're never round the back here with me, getting' it off against the wall because they think I'm tough and good and hard!" He's angry. "No way. They're at home, dreamin' of a Cameron! They're dreamin' of my brother!"

Her voice bruises me.

"Cameron's a loser."

Bruises me hard.

"Yeah, but," Rube goes on, "you know somethin'? He's a loser who walked you home yesterday when I couldn't have cared less. Hell, you could have been beat up or raped for all I cared." His voice batters her, I can feel it. "And there's Cameron, my brother, dyin'

163

like hell to please you and treat you right." He moves her into a corner. "He would too, y' know. He'd bleed for you, and fight for you, without his fists. He'd take care of you and have respect for you and he'd love the hell out of you. You know that?"

It's quiet.

Rube, Steph, door, me.

"So if you wanna do it here with me," Rube jabs her again, "let's go. You're about worth me, but you're not worth him. You're not worth my brother. . . ."

He has swung his last verbal punch now and I feel them standing there. I picture it — Rube looking at her and Stephanie looking somewhere else. Anywhere but at Rube. Soon, I hear her footsteps. The last one sounds like something shattering.

Rube's alone.

He's on one side of the door.

I'm on the other.

To himself, he says, "Always for me." Some silence. "And for what? I'm not really even a . . ." He fades off.

I open the door. I see him.

I walk out and lean back against the wall with him.

I realize that I could have hated him or been jealous

that Steph wanted him instead of me. I could have looked back on her question from last night with bitterness.

Is Rube as good a fighter as everyone says? she'd asked. Yet, I don't feel anything awful. All I can feel is a wish that I'd had the presence of mind to answer something different to her. I should have said, *A good fighter? I don't know — but he's good at being my brother.*

That's what I should have said.

"Hi Rube."

"Hi Cameron."

We lean against the wall and the sun is screaming out in pain on the horizon. The horizon swallows it slowly, eating it up whole. All the city faces it, including my brother and me.

Conversation.

I speak.

I ask, "Y' reckon there really *is* a girl out there like the one y' mentioned? Waiting for me?"

"Maybe."

Fire and blood are smeared across the distant sky. I watch it.

"Really, Rube?" I ask. "Y' reckon?"

"There has to be. . . . You might be dirty and down low, and not much of a winner, but . . ."

He doesn't finish his sentence. He just looks into the evening, and I can only speculate on what he might say, I hope it's something like "but you're big-hearted," or "but you're a gentleman."

Nothing, however, is said.

Maybe the words are the silence.

CHAPTER 14

When you lean against a wall and the sun's setting, sometimes you just stand there and watch. You taste blood but you don't move. Like I said, you let the silence speak. Then you go back inside.

"Twenty bucks' tip money," Perry informs me, handing me a bag when everything's over.

"Huh," I retort. "Pity money."

"No," Perry warns me. He always looks like he's warning you. This time he's telling me to shut up and take the compliment.

"It's pride money," says Bumper. "Walkin' through the crowd like that. They appreciate that more than my win, more than Rube's win, more than all of 'em put together."

I take the money. "Thanks, Perry."

"You've got four more fights," he tells me. "Then your

season's over, right? You deserve the break, I reckon."
He shows Rube and me a sheet of paper that's a competition ladder. In his other hand he holds the draw. On the ladder, he points out where Rube is. "See, you came in three fights late, but you're still on top. You're the only one who hasn't lost a fight."

Rube points at the name sitting on second. "Who's Hitman Harry Jones?"

"You're fightin' him next week."

"He good?"

"You'll drop him easy."

"Oh."

"Look there, he's had two losses. One of 'em was against the bloke you fought tonight."

"Really?"

"Would I say it otherwise?"

"No."

"Well, shut up then." Perry grins. "The semifinals are comin' up in four more weeks." The grin leaves him. Immediately. Now he's serious. "However . . ."

"What?" Rube asks. "What?"

Perry pulls us both aside. He speaks slow and genuine. I've never heard him speak like this. "There's only one slight problem — it's in the last week of the regular comp."

Rube and I both look at the draw closely.

"See it?" Perry sticks a finger on Week Fourteen. "I've decided to be a bit of a bastard."

I see it.

So does Rube.

"Oh man," I say, because right there on the page of Week Fourteen in the lightweight division, it says *WOLFE vs. WOLFE*.

Perry tells us, "Sorry fellas, but I couldn't help it. There's just something about brothers fighting, and I wanted the last week before the semifinals to be memorable." He's still genuine. Just talking business. "Remember, I said there was a slight chance this might happen. You said it wouldn't be a problem."

"You can't rig somethin'?" Rube asks. "You can't change it?"

"No, and I don't want to either. The only good thing is that it's gonna be here, at home."

A shrug. "Well, fair enough then." My brother looks at me. "You got a problem with it Cam?"

"Not really."

"Good," Perry finishes. "I knew I could count on y's."

When everything's packed up, Perry offers us our usual lift home. His voice hammers my mind, as I'm still in pretty bad shape from the beating I copped.

"Nah," Rube tells him. "Not tonight, ay. I reckon we might walk tonight." He goes for my opinion. "Cam?"

"Yeah, why not," even though I'm thinking, *Are you bloody crazy? My head looks like it's gone through a blender.* However, I say nothing more. I think I'll be happy to walk home with Rube tonight.

"No worries." Perry states his position. "Next week boys?"

"Certainly."

We walk out the back door with our gear and tonight there is no one waiting. There's no more Steph, no more anyone. There's only city and sky, and clouds that twirl in the growing darkness.

At home, I hide my battle-bruised face. I have a black eye, swollen cheekbone, and a torn, blood-rusted lip. I eat the pea soup in the sheltered corner of the lounge room.

The next few days fight their way past.

Rube lets his gruff grow a little.

Dad is on the employment trail, as usual.

Sarah goes to work and only goes around to her friend Kelly's place once or twice. She comes home sober and, on Wednesday, with overtime money jammed in her pocket.

Steve comes in once, to iron some shirts.

"Don't you have an iron?" Rube asks him.

"What does it look like?"

"It looks like you don't have an iron."

"Well, guess what, I don't."

"Well, maybe you should go and buy one, y' tighty."

"Who y' callin' tight, boy? How 'bout you go and have a shave. . . ."

"Can't y' afford an iron? This movin' out thing can't be too easy then."

"Damn right. It's not."

The thing is, though, that as they argue, both Steve and Rube are pretty much laughing. Sarah laughs from the kitchen and I smirk in my own juvenile way. This is the sort of thing we specialize in.

Mrs. Wolfe has actually taken the day off work.

What this means is that she has time to notice that there are cuts and bruises healing on my face. As I eat some cornflakes that afternoon, she corners me in the kitchen. I watch her watching me.

She calls out.

One word.

It's this:

"Rube!"

Not too loud. Not panicked. Just a confident strain of voice that expects nothing less than his quick arrival.

She asks, "Is it the boxing training?"

Rube sits down. "No."

"Or have you boys been fighting in the backyard again?"

He confesses a lie.

"Yeah." He's pretty quiet. "We have."

She only sighs and believes us, which is the worst thing. It's always bad when someone believes you when you know they shouldn't. You feel like screaming at them, telling them to stop, so you can live with yourself a little easier.

But you don't.

You don't want to disappoint them.

You can't face your own gutless self and explain that you're not worthy of their trust.

You can't accept that you're that low.

The thing is that we *have* been fighting in the yard, even if it's only practice for the real thing. I guess Rube hasn't exactly lied, but he hasn't told the truth either.

It's close.

I feel it.

I come so close to telling her all about it. Perry, the boxing, the money. Everything. The only thing stopping me now is the bowed head of my brother. Looking at him, I know he's heading somewhere. He's at the edge of something and I can't bring myself to snatch it from under his feet.

"Sorry Mum."

"Sorry Mum."

Sorry Mrs. Wolfe.

For everything.

We'll make you proud another day.

We have to.

We must.

"You know," she begins, "you fellas ought to be looking after each other." Her comment makes me realize that through the lies, the greatest irony is that we *are* looking out for each other. It's just that in the end, we're letting her down. That's what injures us.

"Any luck with work?" Steve asks Dad. I can hear it. They're in the lounge room.

"Nah, not really."

I expect them to begin the usual argument about getting the dole, but they don't. Steve leaves it alone, because he doesn't live here anymore. He only gets a fixed look on his face and says his good-byes. I can tell by his expression that he's thinking, *It'll never happen to me. I won't let it.*

On the Friday of that week, what seems like a typical morning turns out to be a very important one.

Rube and I are out for a run and it's nearly seven when we return. As always, we have our old jerseys, track pants, and gymmies on. The day wears a sky with boulder clouds and a bright blue horizon. At our gate, we arrive and Sarah's there. She asks, "Did y' see Dad while you were out? He's disappeared, ay."

"No," I reply, wondering what the big deal is. "Dad's been taking walks lately."

"Not this early."

Mum comes out.

"His suit's not there," she announces, and instantly, we all know. He's down there. He's waiting. He's gone down to get the dole.

"No."

Someone says it.

Again.

Against the hope that it isn't true.

"No way," and I realize that it's me who has spoken, because the morning-cold smoke has tumbled from my mouth with the words. "We can't let him." Not because we're ashamed of him. We're not. We just know that he's fought this for so long, and we know he sees it as the end of his dignity.

"Come on."

Now it's Rube who has spoken, and he tugs on my sleeve. He calls to Mum and Sarah that we'll be back soon, and we take off.

"Where we goin'?" I pant, but I know the answer, right up until we get to Steve's place. Out of breath from the sprint, we stand there, gather ourselves, then call out.

"Hey Steve! Steven Wolfe!"

People yell out for us to shut up, but soon enough, Steve appears on his apartment balcony in his underwear. His face says, *You bastards.* His voice says, "I thought it was you blokes." Then a shrill, unhappy shout: "What are y's doin' here? It's seven o'clock in the bloody morning!"

A neighbor shrieks, "What the hell's goin' on out there?"

"Well?" Steve demands.

"It's," Rube stutters. "It's Dad."

"What about him?"

"He's . . ." Damn, my voice is still panting. "He's down there." I'm shaking. "Getting the dole."

Steve's face shows relief. "Well, it's about time."

Yet, when Rube and I stare into him, he can tell. We're pleading with him. We're crying out. We're howling for help. We're screaming out that we need all of us. We need — "Ah, bloody hell!" Steve spits out the words. A minute later, he's with us, running in his old football training gear and his good athletic shoes.

"Can't y's run any faster?" he complains on the way, just to repay us for pulling him out of bed and humiliating him in front of his neighbors. He also says through clenched teeth, "I'll get you blokes for this, I promise y's."

Rube and I just keep running, and when we get back to our place, Mum and Sarah are dressed. They're ready. We all are. We walk.

After fifteen minutes, the employment service is in sight. At the doors, there sits a man, and the man is our father. He doesn't see us, but each one of us walks toward him. Together. Alone.

Mrs. Wolfe has pride on her face.

Sarah has tears in her eyes.

Steve has our father in his eyes, and finally, the realization that he would be equally as stubborn.

Rube has intensity clawed across him.

As for me, I look at my father, sitting there, alone, and I imagine his sense of failure. His black suit is a bit short at the ankles, exposing his worn-out socks beneath the pants.

When we get there, he looks up. He's a good-looking man, my father, although this morning, he's defeated. He's broken.

"Thought I'd get down here early," he says. "This is about the time I normally start work."

All of us stand around him.

In the end, it's Steve who speaks. He says, "Hi Dad."

Dad smiles. "Hi Steven."

That's all there is. No more words. Not like you might expect. That's all of it, except that we all know we won't let him do it. Dad knows it too.

He stands up and we resume the fight.

When we walk back, Rube stops at one point. I wait with him. We watch the others walk.

Rube speaks.

"See," he says. "That's Fighting Clifford Wolfe." He points. "That's Fighting Mrs. Wolfe and Fighting Sarah Wolfe. Hell, these days, that's even Fighting Steven Wolfe. And you're Fighting Cameron Wolfe."

"What about you?" I ask my brother.

"Me?" he wonders. "I've been given the name, but I don't know." He looks right at me and says truth. "I've got some fear of my own, Cam."

"Of what?"

What can he be afraid of?

"What will I do when a fight comes along that I might lose?"

So that's it.

Rube's a winner.

He doesn't want to be.

He wants to be a fighter first.

Like us.

To fight a fight he might lose.

I answer his question, to assure him.

"You'll fight anyway, just like us."

"Y' reckon?"

But neither of us knows, because a fight's worth nothing if you know from the start that you're going to win it. It's the ones in between that test you. They're the ones that bring questions with them.

Rube hasn't been in a fight yet. Not a real one.

"When it comes along, will I stand up?" he asks.

"I don't know," I admit.

He'd rather be a fighter a thousand times over among the Wolfe pack than be a winner once in the world.

"Tell me how to do it," he begs. "Tell me." But we both understand that some things can't be told or taught. A fighter can be a winner, but that doesn't make a winner a fighter.

"Hey Rube."

"Yeah."

"Why can't y' be happy bein' a winner?"

"What?"

"You heard me."

"I don't know." He goes over it. "Actually, I do know."

"Well?"

"Well, first, if you're a Wolfe, you should be able to fight. Second, there's only so long you can win for, because someone can always beat you." He draws a breath. "On the other hand, if you learn how to fight, you can fight forever, even when you get belted."

"Unless you give up."

"Yeah, but anyone can stop you being a

winner. Only you yourself can make you stop fighting."

"I s'pose."

"Anyway..." Rube decides to finish it. "Fighting's harder."

CHAPTER 15

like I've said earlier, there are four weeks now until I fight my brother. Fighting Ruben Wolfe. I wonder how it will be, and how it will feel. What will it be like to fight — not in our backyard, but in the ring, under all the lights, and with the crowd watching and cheering and waiting for the blood? Time will tell, I suppose, or at least, these pages will.

Dad's at the kitchen table, alone, but now, my father doesn't look so beaten down. He looks like he's back in it. He's been to the brink and come back. I guess when you lose your pride, even for just a moment, you realize how much it means to you. His eyes have some strength back in them. His curly hair is spiraling at his eyebrows.

Rube's quiet lately.

He spends a fair bit of time down in the basement, which, as you know, has been vacated by Steve. In the end, Mum offered it to everyone for their bedroom, but none of us wanted it. We said it's because it gets so cold down there, but really, I reckon the remaining wolves in our house feel like now's a time to stick together. I've felt it ever since Steve left. Not that I would say it out loud. I would never admit to Rube that I didn't take the basement because I'd get too lonely without him. Or that I'd miss our conversations and the way he always annoys me. Or, as disgraceful as it sounds, that I'd even miss the smell of his socks and the sound of his snoring.

Just last night, I tried waking him, because that snoring of his was dead-set detrimental to my health. Sleep deprivation, I'm telling you. That is, until it gets like a pendulum again, coaxing me into sleep. Huh. Hypnosis under the influence of Ruben Wolfe's snoring. It's hopeless, I know, but you get used to things. You feel weird without them, like you're not yourself anymore.

In any case, it's Mrs. Wolfe herself who has taken hold of the basement. She has a bit of an office down there and does the tax.

On Saturday night, though, I find Rube there instead, sitting on the desk, his feet resting on the chair.

It's the night before his fight with Hitman Harry Jones. I pull the chair from his feet and sit on it.

"Y' right there?" He glares at me.

"I am, yeah. It's a pretty nice chair."

"Don't worry about my feet," he goes on. "They're danglin' now 'cause of you."

"Ah y' poor bloke."

"Got that right."

I swear it.

Brothers.

We're strange.

In here, he won't give me an inch, but out in the world, he'll defend me to the death. The frightening thing is that I'm the same. We all seem to be.

A pause yawns through the air, before Rube and I start speaking without looking at each other. Personally, I look at a blotch on the wall, wondering, *What is that? What the hell is it?* As for Rube, I can sense that he has lifted his feet to the desk and rests his chin on his knees. His eyes, I imagine, are fixed straight ahead, on the old cement stairs.

"Hitman Harry," I begin.

"Yeah."

"You reckon he's any good?"

"Maybe."

Then, right in the middle of it all, Rube says, "I'm gonna tell 'em." His statement brings with it no extra attention, no movement. No prospect of believing that he's thought out what he has said just now. It's been decided long ago.

The only problem is, I have no idea what he's talking about.

"Tell who what?" I inquire.

"Can you really be that thick?" He turns to me now, a savage look on his face. "Mum and Dad, y' yobbo."

"I'm not a yobbo."

I hate it when he calls me that. *Yobbo.* I think I hate it worse than *faggot.* It makes me feel like I'm eating a pie and drinking Carlton Cold and like I've got a beer gut the size of Everest.

"Anyway," he goes on impatiently, "I'm tellin' Mum and Dad about the boxing. I'm sick of the sneakin' round."

I stop.

Think it over in my mind.

"When y' gonna tell 'em?"

"Just before you and me fight."

"Are you crazy?"

"What's wrong with that?"

"They'll keep us from fighting and Perry'll kill us."

"No, they won't." He has a plan. "We'll just promise that it's the last time we'll ever fight each other." Is this part of Rube wanting a real fight? Telling Mum and Dad? Telling them the truth? "They can't stop us, anyway. They might as well see us for what we are."

What we are.

I repeat it, in my head.

What we are . . .

Then I ask it.

"What are we?"

And there's silence.

What are we?

What are we?

The weird thing about the question is that not long ago we knew exactly what we were. It was *who* we were that was the problem. We were vandals, backyard fighters, just boys. We knew what words like that meant, but the words Ruben and Cameron Wolfe were a mystery. We had no idea where we were going.

Or maybe that's wrong.

Maybe who you are *is* what you are.

I don't know.

I just know that right now, we want to be proud. For once. We want to take the struggle and rise above it. We want to frame it, live it, survive it. We want to put it in our mouths and taste it and never forget it, because it makes us strong.

Then Rube cuts me open.

He slits my doubt from throat to hip.

He repeats it and answers it. "What are we?" A brief laugh. "Who knows what they will see, but if they come and watch us fight, they'll know that we're brothers."

That's it!

That's what we are — maybe the only thing I *can* be sure of.

Brothers.

All the good things that involves. All the bad things.

I nod.

"So we'll tell 'em?" He's looking at me now. I see him.

"Yeah."

It's agreed, and I must confess that I myself get obsessed with the idea. I want to run up immediately and tell everyone. Just to let it out of me. Instead, I concentrate on what lies ahead before it. I have three fights of my own to survive, and I must watch Rube fight and the way his opponents fight him. I can't make the same mistakes they make. I've gotta go the distance, and for his sake, I have to give him a fight, not just another win.

To my own surprise, I win my next fight — a points decision.

Right after me, Rube puts the Hitman to bed midway through the fourth round.

The week after, I lose in the fifth, and the last fight before my meeting with Rube is a good one. It's at Maroubra, and compared with my first ever bout there, this time, I walk in and throw punches without hesitating. I'm not scared of being hit anymore. Maybe I've grown used to it. Or perhaps I know that the end is near for me. The guy I'm fighting doesn't come out for the last round. He's too wobbly, and I feel for him. I know how it feels to not want the last round. I know how it feels to concentrate hard on just standing, let alone even thinking about throwing punches. I know how it is for the fear to outweigh the physical pain.

Watching Rube fight later, I see something.

I find out why no one beats him, or why they don't even come close. It's because they don't *think* they can win. They don't believe they can do it, and they don't want it badly enough.

To survive him, I have to believe I can beat him.

It's easier said than done.

"Hey Cam?"

"It's about time."

"About time for what?"

"About time you started the talkin'."

"I've got somethin' important to say."

"Yeah?"

"We'll tell 'em tomorrow."

"Y' sure?"

"Yes. I'm sure."

"When?"

"After dinner."

"Where?"

"Kitchen."

"Okay."

"Good. Now shut up. I wanna get some sleep."

Later, when he starts snoring, I tell him.

"I'm gonna beat you." But personally, I'm not really too convinced.

CHAPTER 16

The money sits on the kitchen table and we all stare at it. Mum, Dad, Sarah, Rube, and me. It's all there. Notes, coins, the lot. Mum lifts Rube's pile up just slightly, to get an idea of how much there is.

"About eight hundred dollars all up," Rube tells her. "That's between Cameron and me."

Mum holds her head in her hands now. Thursday nights shouldn't be like this for her, and she stands and walks over to the sink.

"I think I'm going to be sick," she tells us, bent over.

Dad stands, goes over and holds her.

After about ten silent minutes, they return to the table. I swear, this kitchen table's seen about everything, I reckon. Everything big that's ever happened in this house.

"So how long's this been going on exactly?" Dad throws out the question.

"A while. Since about June."

"Is that right, Cameron?" Mum this time.

"Yeah, that's right." I can't even look at her.

However, Mrs. Wolfe looks at me. "So that's where all those bruises came from?"

I nod. "Yeah." I go on talking. "We did still fight in the backyard, but only for practice. When we started out, we told ourselves that we all needed the money. . . ."

"But?"

"But, I don't think it's ever been about the money."

Rube agrees and takes over. He says, "Y' know Mum, it's just that Cam and I saw what was happening here. We saw what was happening to us. To Dad, to you, to all of us. We were barely surviving, just keeping our heads above water, and . . ." He's getting feverish now. Desperate to tell it right. "We wanted to do something that would lift us up and make us okay again —"

"Even if it makes the rest of us ashamed?" Mum interrupts.

"Ashamed?" Rube boxes her through the eyes. "You wouldn't say that if you saw Cameron fighting, standing up, over and over again." He's nearly shouting. "You'd fall to your knees with pride. You'd tell people that he's your boy and he keeps fighting because that's the way you brought him up."

Mum stops.

She stares through the table.

She imagines it, but all she sees is the pain.

"How can you go through that?" she begs me. "How can you go through it, week after week?"

"How can *you*?" I ask her.

It works.

"And how can you?" I ask Dad.

The answer is this:

We keep getting up because that's what we do. Don't ask me if it's instinct, but we all do it. People everywhere do it. Especially people like us.

When it's nearly all over, I allow Rube to deliver the knockout blow. He does it. He says, "This week is Cameron's last fight." A deep breath. "The only thing is" — a pause — "he's fighting me. We're fighting each other."

Silence.

Total silence.

Then, in all honesty, it's taken quite well.

Only Sarah flinches.

Rube goes on. "After that I've got semifinals. Three more weeks at the most."

Both Mum and Dad seem to be handling it now, slightly. *What are they thinking?* I ask myself. Mainly, I think they feel like they've failed as parents, which is completely untrue. They deserve no blame, because this is something Rube and I did on our own. If we succeeded, it was us. If we failed — us. No blame on them. No blame on the world. We didn't want that, and we wouldn't tolerate it.

Now I crouch down next to my mother. I hug her and tell her, "I'm sorry, Mum. I'm so sorry."

Sorry.

Will that ever do?

Will it ever make her understand enough to forgive us?

"We promise," Rube still tries. "This is the last time Cameron and I will ever fight each other."

"Jeez, that's comforting." Sarah finally speaks. "You can't fight someone when he's dead."

Everyone looks at her and listens, but no one speaks.

It finishes.

A nervous quiet curls through the kitchen air, till only Rube and I sit there. Everyone else leaves. Sarah first, then Dad, then Mrs. Wolfe. Now we wait for the fight.

Living among the next few days, I continue in my determination to believe that I can beat him. I can't pull it off. The closest I come is believing that I *want* to beat him, in order to survive.

When we leave for the warehouse on Saturday night, Mr. and Mrs. Wolfe come with us. Dad makes us all pile into his panel van (with me cramped into the back).

The car takes off slowly.

I sweat.

I fear.

The fight.

My brother.

For my brother — for his own fight.

The whole way there, nothing is said, until we get out at the warehouse, when Dad says, "Don't kill each other."

"We won't."

It's organized in the dressing room that Perry will sit

in Rube's corner. Bumper will be in mine. There's a good crowd.

I can hear it, and I see it, when I go into the *Visiting Fighters* dressing room. I don't look for Mum and Dad because I know they're out there, and I'm concentrating on what I have to do.

In the dirty dressing room, I sit for a while, and other fighters come and go. I walk around. I'm jumpy. This is the biggest fight of my life.

I'm fighting against my brother.

I'm also fighting *for* him. . . .

With a few minutes to go, I lose contact with everyone else. I lie down on the floor. With my eyes shut, my arms at my side. My gloves touch the tops of my legs. I don't see anyone. I don't hear anyone. I'm alone in my mind. There's tension all around me, pressed to the outline of my body. It gets beneath me and lifts me. . . .

I want it, I tell myself. I want it more than him.

Future scenes from the fight angle through my mind.

I see Rube trying to get at me.

I want it.

I see myself ducking and counterpunching.

More.

I see myself, standing, at the end. Standing at the end of a real fight. Not a win, or a loss, but a fight. I see Rube.

I want it more than him, I repeat, and I know that I do. I do want it more, because I have to. I've —

"It's time."

Bumper's near me now, and I jump to my feet and stare forward. I'm ready.

Perry's shouting voice registers, but only for a second. When Bumper pushes through the door, the crowd makes its usual noise. I see it, I feel it, but I can't hear it. I walk on, inside me. Inside the fight.

I climb the ropes.

I get rid of the jacket.

I don't see him, but I know he's there.

But I want it more.

Now.

The ref.

His words.

Silent.

Looking at my feet.

Anywhere but at Rube.

In the suffocating seconds between now and the fight,

I wait. No practice punches, I'll need them all. It's fear and truth and future, all devouring me. It hunts through my blood and I'm a Wolfe. Cameron Wolfe.

I hear the bell.

With it, the crowd comes storming into my ears.

I walk forward and throw the first punch. I miss. Then Rube swings and gets me on the shoulder. There's no slow beginning, no warm-up period or watching time. I move in hard and get underneath. I hit him. Hard on the chin. It hurts him. I see it. I see it because I want it more and he is there to be hurt. He's there to be beaten and I'm the only one in the ring to do it.

It's three minutes per round.

That's all.

Fists and pain and staying upright.

Again, I feel my fist cut through my brother, only this time it rips into his stomach. In reply, a right hand lands on my left eye. We trade punches for nearly the whole round. There's no running, no circling. Just punches. Toward the end, Rube gashes me open. He gets me in the mouth, making my head swarm backward and the pulse in my throat go numb. My legs go, but the round's over. I walk straight to my corner.

I wait.

I want.

The fight is there, and I want Rube to know that he's in it as well. The second round has to convince him.

It begins hard again, with Rube miss-hitting two jabs. I follow, but miss with an uppercut. Rube gets annoyed. He tries to hook me, but it frees him up and I land the best punch of my life on his jaw, and . . .

He staggers.

He staggers, and I chase him to the neutral corner, throwing my fists into his face, and slitting him once over his eye. He finds composure and fights his way out. Nothing hard lands though, and somehow, I stay out of his way the entire round. Once more, I find him on the chin. A good shot. A real good shot, and the round is mine.

"You're in a fight," I tell him. It's all I say, and Rube looks into me.

He comes out even harder in the third, and he gets me on the ropes twice, but only a handful of punches reach their mark. His breathing is heavy and my own lungs are exhausted. When the bell goes, I fake a burst of energy and head straight for my stool. I glance over at

Rube as Perry talks to him. It's the face of our mother when she gets up in the morning, ready for another double overtime shift. It's the face of Dad that day down at the employment service. It's the face of Steve, fighting in his own life and then for his father, simply saying, "Hi Dad." It's the face of Sarah, dragging washing off the line with me. It's my own face, right now.

"He's scared of losin'," Bumper tells me.

"Good."

In the fourth, Rube reacts.

He misses me just once, then opens me up several times. His left hand is especially cruel, pinning me into his corner. Only once do I get through him and clip his jaw again. It's the last time.

By the end of the round, I'm against the ropes, just about gone.

When the bell goes this time, I find my corner, oh, miles and miles away, and stagger toward it. I fall. Down. Into the arms of Bumper.

"Hey buddy," he tells me, but he's so far away. Why's he so far away? "I don't think you can go out for the last. I think you've had enough."

I realize.

"No way," I beg him.

The bell goes again and the referee calls us into the middle. One final handshake before the last round. It's always the same . . . until today.

My head is jolted back by what I see.

Is it real? I ask myself. *Is* . . . because there, in front of me, Rube is wearing only one boxing glove and his eyes circle inside mine. He's wearing one boxing glove, on his left hand, just like all those times in the backyard. He's standing there, before me, and something very slight glimmers across his face. He's a Wolfe and I'm a Wolfe and I will never ever tell my brother that I love him. And he will never tell it to me.

No.

All we have is this. . . .

This is the only way.

This is us. This is us saying it, in the only way we can possibly do it.

It means something. It's about something.

I return.

To my corner.

With my teeth, I take off the left glove. I give it to Bumper, who accepts it in his right hand.

Mum and Dad are somewhere in the crowd, watching.

My pulse does a lap of the silence.

The ref calls something out.

Sight.

Is that what he yells?

No, it's "Fight," although . . .

Rube and I look at each other. He comes forward. So do I. The crowd erupts.

One fist covered. One fist naked.

That's all.

Rube throws first and takes me on the chin.

It's over. I'm hurt, I'm . . . but I throw a punch back, just missing. I cannot go down. Not tonight. Not now, when everything hinges on me staying on my feet.

I'm hit again, and this time the world has stopped. Opposite me, Rube's standing there, wearing a solitary boxing glove. Both his hands are at his side. Another silence gathers strength. It is broken, by Perry. His words are familiar.

"Finish him off!" he calls out.

Rube looks at him. He looks at me. He tells him.

"No."

I find them. Mum and Dad.

I collapse.

My brother catches me and holds me up.

Without knowing it, I'm crying. I'm weeping on my brother's throat as he holds me up.

Fighting Ruben Wolfe. He holds me up.

Fighting Ruben Wolfe. It hurts.

Fighting Ruben Wolfe. His fight inside.

Fighting Ruben Wolfe. Like the rest of us.

Fighting Ruben Wolfe. Not fighting him, no. It's something else. . . .

"Y' okay?" he asks me. It's a whisper.

I say nothing. I just cry on my brother's throat and let him hold me up. My hands feel nothing and my veins are on fire. My heart is heavy and hurting, and out there somewhere, I can imagine the pain of a beaten dog.

I find that nothing more has happened. The bell rings and it's over. We stand there.

"It's over," I say.

"I know," Rube smiles. I feel it.

Even in the following minutes, when scattered money falls into the ring, and when we walk back through the murmuring crowd, the moment carries on.

It carries me back to the dressing room with Rube at my side, as people stare at us and nod and reach out not for Rube or for me, but for this moment that is both of us. "That was some fight," some of them say, but they're wrong. It was more than that. It was Ruben Wolfe and me, and the blood of brothers in our veins.

In the dressing room, the feeling of it helps me get changed, and it waits with me for Rube. When he finds me, Perry arrives as well and sorts out the money, though we both know we'll split it tonight, down the middle. The money means nothing.

On our way out the back door, the crowd roars from another fight, and Perry stops us. I expect him to say something to Rube about not finishing me off, but he doesn't. Instead, with a smile and shake of his head, he says, "Not bad, lads. Not bad at all."

"Thanks," Rube answers, and we walk out.

Tonight, we're pretty quick to leave, mainly for our mother's sake. We meet back at the panel van.

Outside, the cold air slaps me.

We drive home, in silence again.

On our front porch, Mrs. Wolfe stops and gives us each a hug. She hugs our father as well. They both go in.

Standing outside, we still hear Sarah ask from the kitchen, "So, who won?"

We also hear the answer.

"Nobody."

It's Dad.

Mum calls out from inside. "Do you fellas want dinner? I'm heating it up right now!"

"What is it?" Rube answers, hopeful.

"The usual!"

Rube turns to me and says, "Bloody pea soup again. It's a dis-grace."

"Yeah," I agree, "but it's brilliant too."

"Yeah, I know."

I open the flyscreen door and walk into the kitchen. I check out what's going on, and the smell of everyday life fights its way into my nose.

"Hey Rube?"

We're on the front porch, eating pea soup in the dark.

"What?"

"You'll win that lightweight title in a few weeks, won't y'?"

"I'd say so, but I won't be doin' it again next year. I'll tell Perry soon enough." He laughs. "It was pretty good chop there for a while, wasn't it? Perry, the bouts, all of it."

I even laugh myself, for some reason. "Yeah, I guess."

Rube looks in disgust down at his soup. "This is bloody shockin' tonight." He lifts a spoonful and lets it drop back into the bowl.

A car drives past.

Miffy barks.

"We're comin'!" Rube shouts. He gets up. "Here, give us y' bowl."

He takes it inside and when he returns, we make our way off the porch, to get damn Miffy.

At the gate, I stop my brother.

I ask, "What'll y' do when the boxing's over?"

He answers without thinking. "I'm gonna hunt my life down and grab it."

Then we put our hoods on and walk out.

Street.

World.

Us.

Cal's got this thing about fire. It's nothing big at first, just lighting matches, watching them burn, enjoying the calming effects of the flame. It helps him cope with life.

Then he meets Abby, and things start to get out of control. He lets her get close, and she winds him up, playing with him until he thinks he might lose his mind. Suddenly the matches aren't enough.

So Cal comes up with another plan. A bigger plan.

Nothing will ever touch him again. . . .

KEROSENE

by Chris Wooding

THE BEDROOM WAS EMPTY, the sunlight of the late autumn afternoon a pale wash across the crazy-paving pattern of the duvet. A bookshelf stood next to the bed, cluttered with comics, graphic novels, markers, sable brushes, jars full of dirty water, and other assorted odds and ends.

The walls and ceiling were black, but they were painted with a variety of bright cartoons, all following the same motif: clocks. Grandfather clocks, alarm clocks (digital and analog), watches, cuckoo clocks, and more. Some had faces, some were melting in the style of Dalí, and some were blank, with no hands or numerals. Some smiled, some leered, some had teeth, some winked. They floated in a starfield, and a few of them had been captured as they drifted behind another, giving the paintings a curious three-dimensional perspective.

On the wall above the bed hung a clay effigy of a tribal wolf-mask, its flat snout snarling emptily. A wardrobe and a chest of drawers leaned against the other wall, groaning under the weight of the junk that had accumulated on top of them. In the center of the room was a mobile of little wooden baby angels painted brightly with cutesy faces beaming, or with their expressions scrunched up with the effort of blowing their tiny horns. A poster of Larisa Oleynik as Alex Mack was positioned in pride of place opposite the window. A stereo system rested on the floor beside an untidy stack of CDs.

The room was silent.

Then, dimly, there was the sound of a key rattling in a lock downstairs. The latch thudded back, and the front door opened, whining on its hinges. There was a slam as it was closed behind the newcomer, then the sound of footsteps hurrying up the stairs. The door to the bedroom was flung open, and a boy of about sixteen entered, ignoring the "BIOHAZARD" warning sign on the outside. He threw the door closed behind him and slumped down heavily on the edge of the red-and-white bedspread, his head in his hands, breathing hard.

It was a small, thin figure that sat there for a long while, unmoving. His baggy jeans were scuffed and flecked with bright paint. He wore a heavy-knit black sweater that dwarfed his bony shoulders, and a blue T-shirt beneath.

His brown hair stuck out everywhere, an uncontrollable ragtag mop.

"*SHIT!*" he screamed suddenly, his voice sounding raw and high. He sprang off his bed and kicked his chest of drawers hard, sending rolled-up drawings and badges toppling off the edge. Unsatisfied, he laid into it viciously, planting the sole of his battered Converse on it again and again. Next he turned his wrath on the blank face of his wardrobe. He swung a punch into it, his fist driven by a desperate need to hit something, *anything*, to vent the frustration that seared through his veins.

The pain brought him back to his senses. He near broke his knuckles with that first punch, so just to spite himself he threw another one with the same hand. At the last moment, he couldn't help pulling the force out of it. His body was instinctively trying to stop him from harming himself. But it still connected, hard, and the blaze of agony that exploded in his hand almost made him pass out.

His good hand clamped around his wrist, he sat back down on the bed, his teeth clenched while he fought back the urge to cry, ashamed of the tears that pricked at his eyes. The pain in his hand eventually began to subside; the turmoil in his head did not.

It had been one of *those* days. God, it was so *humiliating*. One of those days when he couldn't look anyone in the eye, when he had walked along the road to his house with his attention fixed firmly on the ground in front of his feet, shuffling meekly along so as not to draw attention to himself.

He had been doing alright all day. And then just on the

last stretch, the walk home from the shops, it had all come crashing down on him. He had seen a tall guy with a skinhead wearing tight black jeans and cherry-red Doc Martens, walking along the other side of the road. Mildly interested, he was looking over at him when the guy turned round and met his eye. He had experienced a sudden, unpleasant thrill at being caught staring, and turned his eyes away.

But a moment later, the skinhead had whistled at him, a short, sharp *wheep* through pursed lips. He looked back, feeling a terrified nausea creep into his belly, and the skinhead had flicked him the finger, saying: "You wanna photo, mate? Last longer."

He felt it sweep over him like a cloak. Hot blood flushed into his cheeks, prickling heat across his face and the nape of his neck. His throat tightened at the sides, his heart began to pound, he was sweating, he felt sick. He turned away from the skinhead, looking down, wishing he could disappear. The skinhead didn't hassle him anymore. But the damage was done.

The remainder of the journey was a nightmare. Everyone on the street seemed to be looking at him. It was as if his affliction marked him out, making everyone stare at him. Like some kind of freak. He was conscious of walking fast, but he couldn't help it. He had to get off the street, away from the piercing glares of the passersby.

When he had finally gained the safety of his house, self-disgust had flooded through him. *Why?* Why so afraid?

Afraid? No. *Shy.*

He snorted, smiling bitterly. A sweet word. When people thought of shy, it was always kind of cute. Nice. Coy girls in floral dresses, wide-eyed cartoon squirrels. Not a crippling, awful sensation that made your tongue too thick to speak and locked up your brain. But that was what it meant to him. And it unmanned him, made him pathetic and weak and *ashamed*.

Trembling, he got up and walked unsteadily to the drawers that he had battered seconds earlier. The clocks swam around him in the starfield on the walls. With his good hand, he brought out a box of Swan Vesta matches. Crossing the room, he closed the thick blue curtains, shutting out the dull light, plunging himself into darkness.

He sat back down on the bed and pulled out a match. Slowly, speeding up as he got to the end, he drew it along the sandpaper. It sparked first try, flaring white as the phosphorus head caught, then settling to a steady yellow flame. He watched it, fascinated. Shadows flickered deep on his face in the light of the match. The heat of it was comfort to him. He stared into the heart of the flame, and felt some of the frustration drain out of him. There was peace there, at least.

He let the match burn down, only blowing it out when the pain in his fingertips became too much to bear. He sat there in the darkness for a while, feeling better. Flame was such a calming thing. Just a little match, and he felt okay again.

It was enough. For now.